FORDMATES

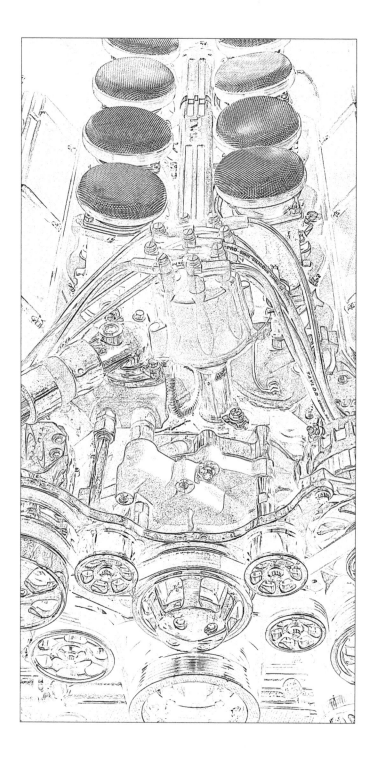

FORDMATES

STORIES FROM THE LINE

IVO MORAVEC

The Porcupine's Quill

Library and Archives Canada Cataloguing in Publication

Title: Fordmates : stories / Ivo Moravec.

Names: Moravec, Ivo, 1948– author.

Identifiers: Canadiana (print) 20230445586 | Canadiana (ebook) 20230445616

   | ISBN 9780889844643 (softcover) | ISBN 9780889844650 (PDF)

Classification: LCC PS8626.O73485 F67 2023 | DDC C813/.6—dc23

1   2   3   •   25   24   23

Published by The Porcupine's Quill, 68 Main Street, PO Box 160,

Erin, Ontario NOB 1TO. http://porcupinesquill.ca

Edited by Stan Dragland. Represented in Canada by Canadian Manda. Trade orders are available from University of Toronto Press.

We acknowledge the support of the Ontario Arts Council and the Canada Council for the Arts for our publishing program. The financial support of the Government of Canada is also gratefully acknowledged.

Canada Council Conseil des arts
for the Arts du Canada

ONTARIO ARTS COUNCIL
CONSEIL DES ARTS DE L'ONTARIO

an Ontario government agency
un organisme du gouvernement de l'Ontario

Canadä

Ontario

In memory of Bód'a
& for the guys and gals with
whom I shared the line

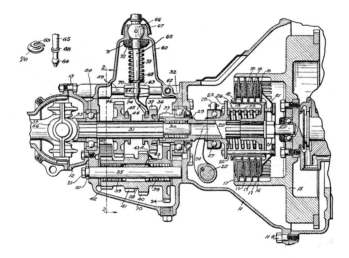

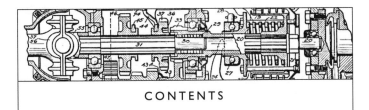

CONTENTS

THE GREENHORN

Welcome, wanderer, to our neck of this lovely plant, welcome. My name is Robert, or just Rob. I will be your guide and instructor for the next three days. After that, you will be my successor. I will put this driveshaft into your hand and flee, and you will be bound to this spot like the ferryman who was bound to his boat in the story. You will stay here, waiting for the next wanderer to take this oar, I mean driveshaft, into his hands, so you, too, might run for your life.

Your very first day in the plant! A veritable greenhorn! My congratulations on getting hired—and my condolences for the same. Don't look at me like that. I'm just trying to be witty.

We've got three days for your training, so there's no need to rush. I could train you in a day—this is not a complicated job—but the rules give us three days and we would be silly not to use them all.

You're lucky they sent you here. You'd be much worse off in the body shop. Plenty of really hard jobs there. Driveshaft is not the worst of the killer jobs. There's some lifting, yes, but it's a relatively slow job, so you don't have to hustle all the time. You'll have some moments to catch a breather. Just watch me doing the job for a while, and then I'll teach you step by step. In the meantime, let me tell you something about this plant of ours, so you can get your bearings and find your way around the belly of the beast you've landed in. I will be your guide in this verbal tour around our magical realm, with its blend of technology, economics, and humanity.

I don't think it's fanciful to call this assembly plant a magic kingdom. Well, of course *kingdom* would be too big a word for our plant, since Mr Ford's kingdom is worldwide. Being only a small part of it, we might be, let's say, a duchy. Magic duchy also sounds good, doesn't it? Well, yes, magic. There must be some powerful magic at work to conduct a huge pile of parts through a thousand pairs of hands, conjuring a new car, a car that comes alive with the turn of a key, by the end of line eight. Yes. Only magic can achieve that. When you leave today, stop at line eight and have a look. This coming alive happens six hundred times every shift. Beware, though. Magic both good and bad is present here. The bad magic feeds an opposite process. It can separate a human being into biological parts and drive out the animating spirit.

Our magic duchy spreads over who knows how many acres. I've never been able to remember the exact number, but I know it's about six times bigger than the Vatican. It stretches from the body and paint shop facing the midnight side to the shipping line on the south end. Under our roof, we have three railway stations, not to mention a number of loading docks to accommodate the big trucks that deliver all the parts and material. Outside is a railway station for loading the finished cars. The part of the line we're on now is called chassis, and it is part of the third line. It's the longest one in the plant, stretching for about three hundred metres. As you can see, the line here has the shape of two parallel, oversized bicycle chains, about a metre apart. In other zones, the line takes a different form: on the engine line, for instance, engines move suspended from rails; in trim, whole cars float along on suspended jaw-like carriers. The shape of the line is meant to facilitate the best possible access for the people who work there.

If you lift your eyes above the line, you will not see the sky. We are in the realm of technology, of around-the-clock artificial light. Our sun and stars are of a technological nature. A sort of canopy stretches above us. The chaotic latticework above the lines is not a system of tree branches, but of rails and beams on which different fixtures, hoists, guns, and balancers hang and roll. Those red spirals are the pressurized air hoses that power the guns. Everything that tightens bolts or nuts, or drives screws, is called a gun. Some guns are small, like the one I'm using, and they look like real handguns. The bigger ones look more like field hockey sticks or even small bazookas. Depends on the job. Some guns can tighten several bolts at once. Most hang within easy reach, just above the head of an operator, and are held in proper position by a spring called a balancer. Your overhead view is completed by a number of yellow fans, three feet across. They do look like small suns. They come in real handy in the summer.

Our zone of the line is hugely important, maybe even the most important zone of all. It's the heart of the whole factory. Three mighty streams, three major lines, have their confluence here. If you make an about-face, you will see a mighty frame line rolling in from the south. At its beginning, there's nothing but a bare black frame, just a skeleton of future underbody. As it's carried down the line, the skillful hands of our mates on this line put into place rear axles, A-frames to hold the front wheels, coil springs, shocks, brake rotors and calipers, brake lines and fuel lines, most of the exhaust, and steering boxes with the whole steering linkage, not to mention many other parts. Then, as you can see, the whole frame is lifted into the air and transferred to our side of the aisle. Rick, master of the descent, lowers the frame down from above and settles it right into the V-shaped saddle he has placed across the line. That will carry the frame to the end of this line. Our job is to attach the driveshaft to the differential so that Gary and Sam over there can arrange a rendezvous with the engine line. A line of engines, coupled with transmissions and equipped with all the starters and alternators and power pumps and radiator hoses, is descending from higher spheres. Sam hooks an engine onto his hoist and pushes it above the line where Gary inserts the end of our driveshaft into a transmission, and then both of them together deck the whole eight-hundred-pound, eight-cylinder monster gently into the frame. And just a little bit further down …

But here comes our relief man, and we are on break. Twenty minutes. The breaks are staggered because the line never stops except for lunch. This guy, Tony, is master of six jobs. He goes from one operator to the next, covering their jobs while they're on break. Today we have fifth break, tomorrow it'll be fourth, then third, and so on. The first two breaks are fifteen minutes, the rest twenty minutes. After that, Tony takes his break, then starts his second round. Those who got fifteen minutes in the first round will now get twenty, and we'll get fifteen. So, you're free for twenty minutes. Sit somewhere and rest. The toilets are this way, above the line. You reach them by climbing those stairs. One cafeteria is over there, beyond line one. We have a small unit here, just vending machines for drinks, coffee, chips, and some chocolate bars. You can sit over there if you're tired of the noise. It's quiet there. Unless some joker like me grabs a fistful of bolts and tosses them against the windows. It makes a real racket when nobody is expecting it, so it startles everybody. More often than not they spill their coffee or even choke on it. No, the windows won't break—they're plastic. Why startle those people? To have some fun. Working on the line, you have to goof around a bit to prevent your mind from going goofy.

And now you're going to do some work. I'll bring in and place the driveshaft and you'll grab the gun with the long barrel that's hanging here with its handle up, upside down like a bat, yes, grab it with your left hand, while the right hand scoops three bolts out of this box. Load one bolt into the socket, find the hole at the end of the driveshaft, pull the trigger, and screw it to the differential. Load the next bolt and repeat. If the third hole is at the bottom or difficult to access, just give the driveshaft a half turn with your right hand. See, it's easy. You're doing fine.

So, where did we finish our tour? Yes, the next big confluence.

Your eye can't miss those colourful, shiny bodies running parallel to and above our line before descending on the underbody, some fifty metres away. When a body and an underbody reach exactly the right position, hydraulics start pushing the whole underbody, with engine, up into the body. Two guys make sure the fit is precise, then secure the connection, first with two bolts. The bodies have had a long journey, too—the longest one, when you think about it. They start in the body shop as pressed-out floor panels. Then the side pillars and firewall and back panel are welded to it, followed by the roof and fenders, then a hood and deck lid, and the doors are screwed to the hinges. Then the whole body gets a dip in an e-coat tank and a bath in a pool with rustproofing stuff, followed by a bath in another pool with base colour. Finally, the skillful hands of paint shop mates spray the whole body with three layers of colour. After some time in heat treatment ovens, they rest in the mezzanine to cool off.

Pa da da da daaa da da … rock 'n' roll, baby! The expression on your face just made my day. Did you think I'd snapped? Nothing to worry about. I know perfectly well that this driveshaft is not my guitar. It's just, well, a good rock riff flashed through my mind, and I had to 'play' it. I do delight in throwing people off balance. You're right, I've played guitar for must be almost thirty years. Before my teens, I didn't learn much. I hated the exercises. I preferred to be outside, hitting a baseball or chasing a tennis ball or a puck in winter. I learned just the basics of guitar, but that paid off handsomely later. At eighteen, I started playing in a rock band. It was cool back then. As soon as I started performing, I knew exactly why it was cool. I tell you, man, a rock band is a gold mine. It's not the money. We were just a local band, playing for small change or, more often, just for the hell of it. But. It has been proven, over and over again, that a young man standing on a stage and playing an electric guitar is much more attractive to girls than the same guy standing in the audience. Why? Don't ask me. I never gave it a thought. Ask those teenage girls. All I know is that rock bands are chick magnets. On a local level. That was good enough for me. Got me plenty of girls at the age when a guy's life orbits around girls, and that counts for a hell of a lot. Good times… very good.

Look at you. My reminiscences are making you dreamy. Daydreaming is not good when you're learning a new job. You might start inserting just one bolt instead of the three. Back to work. Where did we finish our plant tour? Oh, yes. At the paint shop, where the car bodies are resting.

During the ride on lines one and two, the bodies are equipped with the inside cabin roof, the dashboard, all the electrical harnesses and wiring, the radiator, heating and air-conditioning, locking mechanisms wherever those are needed, the gas tank, and about two dozen other necessities. On our line, all those elements have to be connected. Our line could easily be nicknamed the wedding line, because here occurs a mating of the parts that have been waiting, longing for each other. The driveshaft slides into the transmission, the fuel line is hooked up to the gas tank at one end and the fuel pump at the other. Hoses are pushed over the radiator intakes. No, of course this is not my usual way of speaking, I'm just being playful now, to spice up your tour. Normally, I don't talk much. Gary and Sam work too far away, and Rick prefers listening to his Walkman, so I have nobody but myself to talk to. The workstations are too far apart for a sustained chatting. We touch through our work, not words. It's a big place and you know maybe five or six people, working close to you, by name. Others are just nameless figures and faces. In a sense, despite two thousand friendly Fordmates around you, this can be a lonely place. I spend too much time in my own mind, and the pressure has been building. Now here you are, my audience, and the words are spurting out of me like rocks from a volcano. They're irrepressible. If you mind, pal, that's your bad luck. I'm going to lay it all on you whether you like it or not. The urge is stronger than I am.

What comes next, after our line? The car is carried overhead to lines four through seven—the lines called trim—and there the work-in-progress gets seats, sound isolation, carpets, safety belts, windows, door panels, outside mirrors, headlights and taillights, that kind of stuff. Jobs on those lines are mostly good—no heavy lifting like we have here or on the frame line. On line eight they do windshields, wiper blades, lots of cosmetics, then pump in all the fluids, including gas. At the end of the line, the finished car is started and driven to the rolls test. It also passes through the alignment station and the water test on the way to the shipping line. That's it. We started with nothing but a pile of parts, now there's a brand-new luxury car. A miracle. Magic. Now the car is driven outside, loaded on a railway car. It heads out into the world. Altogether, this magical transformation takes about twenty-seven hours, including time when the car is not being worked on. It takes fifteen hundred people and at least twice that many parts. You can have one. It'll cost you about ten months' wages. That would translate into … let me think, yes, about a hundred and twenty thousand installed driveshafts.

Well, you've mastered the gun part of the job, so we can tackle the worst part. Now you'll start hurting. Here we have two baskets with two types of driveshaft. These ones are for the regular Crown Victorias and Grand Marquises, and those ones are heavy duty, for police and taxi versions. The shafts are colour-coded with those three pink and purple stripes. To know which one to install, you check this piece of paper, see, that comes taped to every frame. It's called a teletype, and it gives you the specs for each car. You check only this one square. N is for normal, D is for heavy duty. Is that clear? Those baskets with the driveshafts rest on hydraulic tables so you can raise them as the basket gets emptier. It's best to adjust the height often so as to keep the edge of the basket at the same level as the incoming frame. Then you can swing the driveshaft more or less horizontally, without having to lift it too much. Grab the driveshaft from this side, facing up the line, then a half turn of your body should be enough to bring it to the frame. Make sure you turn with your whole body by stepping sideways, not with your torso only, or you'll screw up your back in no time.

See the red dot at the end of the driveshaft? The same dot is on the differential. Bring them together and your bolt holes will be aligned. So, let's try it. I'll do the bolts. How much does a driveshaft weigh? They say about twenty-five pounds. In the morning. By noon it's about thirty-five and it gets heavier as the day goes on. I guess it absorbs humidity from the air.

What did you do for a living before Ford? Delivered pizza? Well, that might train maybe your legs, but you'll have to get used to some heavier lifting. You'll suffer, my boy, you will. Your back, of course. During a single shift, you'll lift and carry about seven thousand kilograms, half of it bending forward to the basket or over the frame. I guarantee you some back pain, but that'll be only muscles. That's why I'm telling you to avoid twisting your waist—the last thing you want is to screw up the vertebrae in your spine. In the first months, your shoulders and forearms are going to howl in protest. So will your wrist, from turning the driveshaft. Even your legs will get tired. Standing for ten hours can be quite taxing. Brace yourself for six weeks of hell. But you can get used to all that over time. You'll become more relaxed. For one thing, your muscles will be trained and they'll get stronger; for another, you'll get used to a certain level of pain. After three months, you should be fine.

How to escape from this job? The fastest way is to throw in the towel, just go home and stay there. The more usual way takes a lot of patience. When Ford hired you, they assigned a number which tells everybody that you were, let's say, the twelve thousand and fiftieth worker hired in this plant since day one. Whenever there is a job vacant you can bid on it. Lowest number gets the job, because its bearer has been around the longest. But my guess is that you'll be stuck on this job for about a year. Then the new greenhorns will come in, and you'll move one step up on the seniority ladder.

Well, it's almost five o'clock. Go home. I'll finish the shift myself. Soak yourself in a tub of hot water. Have a beer to sleep well. Get some rest. Tomorrow it'll start getting worse.

Now you've learned both parts of the job, so we'll alternate: half an hour on driveshafts, half an hour gunning the bolts. What would you like to start with? How badly are you hurting? Not that much? Good for you. Now listen, and chisel what I tell you into your mind because this is crucial: you are now in the probation period. Ninety days. The collective agreement is a deal between the Union and the Company, but as you will not become a Union member until after ninety days, it doesn't really cover you. It means that during those three months, the Union is not protecting you. It is believed that the Company can kick you out at any time, with or without a reason. I don't want to scare you, just make sure you're aware of the dangers you are about to face. The pain will get worse, much worse. After three or five weeks on the job, your whole body will hurt so much that you'll howl like a pack of jackals. You can howl to your buddies here as much as you like, but it doesn't make a good impression if you go to your family doctor, or to Medical here. Who knows, it might suggest to the Company that you can't hack it—and earn you an immediate homeward bound kick in the butt. Even if you have to crawl home on all fours, you have to keep going. If you are so weak and sore that you can't so much as lift a slice of pizza, or a piece of bread, or a bottle of beer, ask somebody at home to spoon-feed you. Drink your beer with a straw. If you wake up with fingers curled like talons, soak them in hot water. For your back and other muscles, I recommend a hot bath and RUB A535 cream. A massage, if you have somebody to do it. If you're so stiff in the morning you can't get out of bed, ask somebody to drag you up and drive you here and push you through the gate. Once inside the plant, the atmosphere, the air, the noise, the line, they'll all boost your strength somehow. Habit will take over. You'll catch up, and you'll survive each shift on sheer willpower. Do whatever works for you, but for ninety days, forget the word *doctor* unless you have a really serious injury. After that you can be at Medical twice a day, because the Union will be standing behind you. That's what the probation period is for. A test of how much you can endure. It is survivable. I survived it. So did Gary and Sam. Over three thousand people have managed to survive it. And there are worse killer jobs than the driveshafts.

Okay, now try to do the whole job. I'm here to help you out if something goes wrong. See, it's easy. Keep going.

Where am I headed on tiptoe? I want to surprise Gary. His big cardboard box with body pucks is almost empty, so he has to lean inside to get the last few. I sneak behind the box, and, at the right moment, when he has his head inside, I smack the cardboard with this stick. It makes a loud boom. He jumps, he curses, and we all have a little fun. He'll wonder how to get even with me, which will give him something to think about for a while. Why do I do this? To make sure something more exciting than the damned driveshafts is happening around here. I told you, you either goof around or your mind goes goofy. Everybody comes up with some stupid idea or another. Some stage fights with gloveballs. Gloveballs? You'll need to know about this. Take two dirty gloves, especially the knitted kind, lay them flat on a surface, one on top of the other. From the tips of the fingers, roll them together, all the way up to the wrists. Pull the wrist band over the ball to prevent unrolling. You roll your socks together before deposit them in your drawer, right? Same idea. Aim, throw, laugh. Now and then, in the summer heat, some-body will grab a fire extinguisher and start sprinkling everybody with water. Occasionally, you'll hear somebody yell at the top of his lungs, or howl, or sing, or yodel. No, they aren't crazy—probably not, anyway—they're just feeling a surge of playfulness in the midst of this drudgery. It's a brief, tiny rebellion against the dictates of technology, against the damn almighty line that runs and runs and runs.... Remember, if you're going to throw a gloveball, you have to throw it in pretty much a horizontal line. Otherwise, it'll get caught up in the tangle of guns and air hoses above the line and never reach your target.

Wow, that was excellent. You've been going for twenty minutes without a single mishap. Now it's my turn. In the meantime, turn on this flashing light to call the forklift guy to bring us a fresh basket of driveshafts. You can open the basket. Then sit and have a rest.

It's well worth enduring the three months of probation, because your resilience will bring you plenty of benefits—and not just those covered by our collective agreement. Informal benefits, unspoken ones. The word *Ford worker*, or *Fordmate*, as I call our guys and gals, has a proud ring to it. Being a Fordmate means being somebody. Banks will be elbowing each other to offer you a substantial mortgage, just because you work at Ford. Your reputation with women will get a considerable boost, probably because we Fordmates have the reputation of being tough guys. Rightly so, I should say. Wimps run away immediately or don't last long. Our jobs keep us in top physical shape. A fitness center like Nautilus is a kids' playground compared to the line. Strong muscles, thick wallet: an unbeatable combo.

But you'd better be careful. I can think of one woman, such a darling—she's divorcing her third Fordmate to marry a fourth. All within twenty years. With each divorce, she's been after the money, but not only that. It's a bigger deal that she gets half of the guy's pension for the years he spent with her. She has already qualified for a Ford pension worth ten years of working here. If she keeps this racket going till she's sixty-five, she'll have a Ford pension as if she had worked on the line for twenty years, without ever having set foot in the plant!

We have three femmes fatales working on the line. Beauties, I suppose. Those ones are not after money or pension. After all, they work at Ford. But they seduce married fellow workers for sport.

Who knows why? To prove to themselves how irresistible they are? Delayed puberty? Revenge? I don't know. Maybe all this strategy of plotting and daydreaming keeps their minds busy on the line. On the other hand, there's a girl in the cafeteria with dimples in her cheeks when she smiles. She looks at you with longing eyes and has been overheard a few times saying, wistfully, 'There's sixty feet of dick on the line and I can't get six inches.' Well, as you can see, there are some risks attached to being a Fordmate.

No, I don't seduce girls with my guitar anymore, though I still play with a band. Once you're a part of that scene, there's no way out. But priorities change. Good buddies, lots of fun. Lady Music is always elusive and intriguing. The wild years are gone with the seasons, just like in those old songs. Girls have retreated into the background. Now they're just the audience. Also, they're a generation younger. Even though, now and then, you can see in their eyes that you could, if you wished.... Not me, not anymore. I've been lucky enough to marry a wonderful woman and have three children. I'm not going to wreck all that because some teenager is charmed by our rendition of a Guns N' Roses song. Not me, no sir. These days I turn to my guitar mostly because playing stirs something up, gets my mind going, makes me feel alive. It's a potent antidote to the mind-deadening effects of the line.

Well, well, well, our third day is almost over. You've been trained and initiated. Tomorrow, the weight of the job falls on your shoulders alone. See, the line is down and the buffer on the frame line is empty, so it'll take at least four minutes before the next frame reaches us. Sit down. I brought a couple of beers in my lunchbox to finish your training in style. No, it's not allowed, but if nobody sees you.... To your successful mastery of the driveshafts!

I've told you so much over these three days that your head must be twice its normal size and buzzing like a beehive, but I can't resist offering you one more bit of wisdom. When you win the physical battle in three months' time—and, having watched you,

I believe you will—the victory will elate you and sustain you for half a year, maybe even a full year. Then, slowly, sneakily, almost imperceptibly, boredom will start fogging your mind like morning mist. That's the moment to blow the bugle again, because that's when another fight begins. A far worse enemy than physical pain is at the gates. The real battle of the Ford assembly line, day in, day out, will now be upon you. You'll have to fight for your spiritual life. The line will try to limit it, take it away, annihilate it, carry it off into the void. You'll have to find something to keep your spirit afloat. Almost everyone here has a hobby or passion or ambition that keeps them sane. I make practical jokes so we can laugh a bit. And I have my music. We have a wonderfully artistic carver, a sculptor who can carve a tree trunk into a real statue. Another is an amateur blacksmith who forges custom-made hunting knives. I've met an immigrant who every day brings a piece of paper with long lists of English words to learn, so as to expand his vocabulary. Quite a few people around here restore antique cars or furniture. Plenty of people coach children's baseball and hockey, or referee games. Collect stamps, raise aquarium fish, make up new recipes, write poetry, invent a new kind of wheel, or some perpetuum mobile—whatever strikes your fancy—but keep your mind busy and simmering with ideas, because the line will do its best to empty it out completely. It'll try to erase you as a thinking human being and turn you into its robotic appendage.

I'm not joking. I'm not trying to be witty now. The struggle is not just to land or keep this well-paying and relatively secure job. It's about you, about who you really are. Do you have it in you to fight to your last breath, or will you run off after being hit by the first blow? Have you got enough moral backbone to mobilize your last ounce of energy and willpower to survive, even though you're taking beating after beating? Are you a fighter or a quitter? Can you wrestle some bit of freedom from the line? Do you need freedom at all? One way or the other, those first three months, then that next year, or the two or three after that, will make an indelible imprint in your soul. It's good to know beforehand what's at stake, what you're playing for, and against what odds.

Dammit, the line is moving again. I'll cover the last few minutes till the buzzer goes today and I say goodbye to the job. Go home and get ready for tomorrow. Be ready for all hell to break loose. Good luck. Rock and roll, baby Fordmate. I'll be rooting for you.

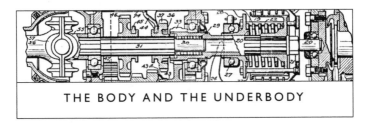

THE BODY AND THE UNDERBODY

The general foreman stuck his index finger in the air to conclude his shit-kicking, then drove away. Ronnie, the supervisor of our line and the recipient of Morgan's bullying, was downcast. Calls of 'Heads are gonna roll!' greeted Ronnie as he returned to the line.

Instead of joining in on the chirping as usual, Andy spat, frowning, at Morgan's disappearing back. 'Bastard! I'd like to see anybody handle this shitty line better than this greenhorn.'

'Is it true,' I asked, 'that when he started working here, Ronnie wanted to try out every job on every line?'

'Yeah, he's been an enthusiast. Until the Union slowed him down with seniority rules. But he got the better of them. He spent all his breaks exploring every job he could.'

'What is he, nuts?' I was amazed by the unusual account of workaholism.

'Nothing to worry about, unless it comes to …' And Andy roared with laughter. 'Do you know Tina? The redhead on line seven? She told me that Ronnie took her out for dinner on a Saturday night. After the second beer, he told her how he felt about the beauty of body decking, when the pistons push the underbody into the shiny new body. After the fourth beer, he was getting passionate about details of the hydraulics, and after the seventh he swore that he felt like an indispensable part of the miracle that turns a pile of auto parts into a glittering luxury car with a crown on its hood. She told me he looked real solemn, like a prophet or a politician. She didn't have the heart to bring him down to earth by making a pass at him. She just got really nicely drunk.'

'Now I know he's nuts. Mind you, it's a lucky guy who can keep his spirits up though this moronic drudgery. The rest of us just work and eat and sleep.'

'But I really don't like the way Morgan breathes down his neck.' Andy pointed at Ronnie's stooped shoulders. 'Another month like this, I bet Ronnie flushes his walkie-talkie down the toilet and away he goes.' Andy was pointing somewhere beyond the engine line, in the general direction of the psychiatric hospital. 'We've got to cheer him up a bit,' he added, and turned on his flasher.

Ronnie went into his famous forward slant then froze. Another red light had come on, and it wasn't just flashing, like ours, because the line had stopped. He about-faced and darted off towards the greater of the two calamities.

Somewhere in some office, a computer registered every second that a line didn't move, accumulating proof of each supervisor's incompetence. Every minute of downtime cost the Company five thousand dollars, and every supervisor felt these penalty minutes as if they were five thousand bucks worth of quarters and dimes hanging from his neck. Every supervisor feared that, one day, the master of this computer would come to confiscate the tokens of his power: the jacket with the Ford logo and his name embroidered on the left breast pocket, and—most of all—the walkie-talkie, the troubleshooter's six-gun. After all, only a rookie tried to solve a problem; a seasoned guy knew to call somebody and pass the buck. Visions of being demoted, of being reduced to wearing the common blue coveralls of the line, haunted the supervisors so relentlessly that they often ended up in the house with knobless doors. In most cases, a good rest erased the 'in' from insane and they came back to supervise some other zone of the line, their fears reinstated along with them to haunt them some more. But Ronnie hadn't succumbed to the stress. Yet.

Now the line began to move again, and Ronnie sprinted toward us from behind a four-level stock rack. From a distance he began to gesture, and we could read the crucial question in his eyes: 'You didn't mismatch the engine, did you?'

Andy put on a funereal look and kept talking to me. 'If it was up to me, I'd subsidize supervisors to visit that new cabaret with the table dancers, let them unwind a bit. It'd be good prevention and cheaper than workers' compensation.'

'What the hell is going on here?'

Andy quietly finished what he was doing, took off his glove, and shook Ronnie's hand. 'I've been watching you since you took over our line, and I have to say that you are doing a superb job. Congratulations!'

Ronnie would have killed Andy on the spot if he'd had a replacement available. But before he could visualize all the appropriate variants of death, he felt himself relaxing. Andy had a reputation for being a bit of practical joker, but this little diversion had none of the hallmarks of his harmless pranks. So he just glared daggers at Andy who, miraculously, survived and didn't even laugh victoriously at catching Ronnie off guard.

'Ronnie, I'm serious. Don't be so tense all the time. It's the tension that'll get you. Surely you don't think that a little fart like you is going to avert a real disaster. Hell, no. The best thing you can do is maintain a sense of humour. Laugh a little.'

'Ha ha ha,' said Ronnie, his mind already on his next task. 'No more fooling around. It's tour day.' He sauntered a few steps before picking up speed on the way to deal with another emergency. Probably a quality controller's rubber-stamp pad had dried up.

'I'd be sorry if he snapped,' Andy remarked. 'This job means a lot more than money to him. He really loves it. He's one of the few.'

'Put on your Sunday-best coveralls! The visitors are coming,' bellowed Peter, swerving his forklift around the corner with a new batch of vinyl roofs.

'Right after you shoe-shine your safety boots!' Andy yelled back, pretending indifference. But I knew he was going to comb his mane. He, like me, always pretended to ignore the tour groups gawking at us, but we both liked the opportunity to show off our virtuosity.

We enjoyed stepping out of anonymity once in a while, if only to disprove the misconception that cars just appeared from nowhere, fully formed, as if hatched by dealerships. No, it's us. It's Andy and me who make the cars. Enjoy this concerto for four hands. Savour the elegance with which Andy hoists up an eight-hundred-pound eight-cylinder motor. Relish the ease and precision of the single move of my wrist directing the U-joint to insert the driveshaft into the transmission. Watch as, together, we gently swing the whole powertrain up into the frame, like tucking a baby into a cradle. Don't you feel as though you are at the ballet, ma'am? Are you not impressed by our feats of strength and skill? Ours is the toughest and most beautiful job at the whole plant.

Ronnie reappeared full speed, waved off Andy's invitation for more chatter, and dove between two huge boxes with body pucks on the other side of the line. He practically flew to answer the phone. So he didn't see Andy's eyes suddenly widening.

'Holy smokes!' he exclaimed.

I swivelled my head to behold two beauties leading the tour group. Both girls were a testament to the artistic talents of Mother Nature, from their Madonna-like faces to their slim ankles; they were supremely rounded in all the appropriate places. As they walked with grace and dignity, a slight jiggle hinted at the absence of bras.

I could see Andy's hand grasping empty air instead of the hoist controller he had grasped half a million times, and I knew it was because his eyes and mind were drowning in that tidal wave of feminine charm. Finally, he succeeded in hooking up the engine and I was reaching for it with my left arm when he froze. Together, at that moment, we might have constituted a life-size realistic sculpture entitled *The Engine Age*, suitable for installation in the lobby of Ford's world headquarters. The size of Andy's eyes made me turn my own head. One of the women had rolled up her T-shirt over her face, as if she wanted to play peekaboo with Andy. It wasn't until she pulled her shirt down that the spell broke. Andy blinked several times, awakened, and finished hooking up the engine. I shook my head and joined him. We barely managed to finish that car before it passed beyond the reach of our hoist. Andy reached for the next engine, then stiffened once again. Once more his hand was waving through space and I knew at once that the girl must have been overcome by shyness and covered her face with her shirt once again. By the time she had mercy and covered herself, Andy had lost all interest in engines. With one jump, he reached for the switch. The red light went on and the line stopped.

The other guys had been working along in the usual manner, mentally wandering in more pleasurable realms, their bodies on autopilot. With the line stopped, they roused from their stupor and looked up. Graced with a larger audience, the girl repeated her performance. The effect was so powerful that everyone stood transfixed. A beastly howling sounded from behind a rack, but it was only Ronnie, who had just discovered that the line was down again.

Inspired by her friend, the other beauty pulled the hem of her skirt up to her waist, did a quick flash and then let the skirt slip back into place. There was a logo printed on her panties: Lemelin's, a new gentleman's establishment a couple of minutes down the road from the plant. Then she stepped out of the skirt altogether, picked it up and twirled it above her head, swinging her hips to the hard rock coming from the radio playing up the frame line. Not to be outdone, the first one pulled her skirt down too, but she was wearing neither logo nor panties, and it so happened that Ronnie burst upon the scene to the view of a nude female rear end, a view so totally unexpected that at first he couldn't quite grasp what he was seeing.

'Why's the line down?' he barked at Andy.

Andy didn't think any words were necessary and just pointed to the dancing girl.

'Start the line!' yelled Ronnie.

'I refuse. On the grounds of safe ...'

The moment the women's dancing caused their bellies and breasts to face us was the moment Ronnie finally understood. The girls were laughing and inviting us to come over to Lemelin's, where, they promised, we would see much, much more! They paid no attention to Ronnie ordering them out of the plant. He looked about ready to get on his knees and beg when an avalanche of yelling issued from his walkie-talkie. It was Morgan demanding to know why the damned line was down again. Ronnie stammered something about buttocks and breasts, and it was easy to imagine Morgan, on the other end, concluding that another supervisor had just gone round the bend. Ronnie was trembling now, either for fear of Morgan's wrath or with incomprehension at the incongruity of such eroticism on display at his place of work. Possibly it was both. I had a pretty good idea what was running through his mind: there's nothing in the supervisor's manual explaining how to handle almost nude girls on the line. No guidelines at all! Just over and over again—one minute of downtime equals five thousand bucks. I could all but see the digits flashing before his inner eye, faster and faster against the background of those lovely cavorting girls, flashing like digits on a gas bar display. Thousands, tens of thousands! I understood why he showed no reaction at all when Morgan arrived with an entourage of assorted foremen and experts. One glance at the situation told Morgan that his supervisor would be able to provide no useful information. He pushed through the circle of spectators, evaluated the situation, and thundered: 'Get your clothes on and get out!'

'But we haven't got all our clothes off yet,' one of the girls retorted sweetly, though that wasn't quite true. One of them, at least, was naked.

Morgan savoured the presentation for a few seconds, then let company loyalty wrest control from his libido. He started to roll up his sleeves. The crowd roared, thinking he was going to join the show, but no, he had nothing so appropriate in mind. He was just preparing to drag the girls out bodily. Thanks to his stoutness, the girls managed to play tag with him for a few moments before they got scared.

'Don't touch!' they screamed. 'Do *not* touch! It would be … sexual assault!'

Morgan had no desire to wiggle at the end of that line in court. He just rolled down his sleeves and walked to the switch in hopes that the guys would start working if he got the line moving. But the guys were all shouting: 'It's not safe … it's a question of safety … our health is at stake!' which gave Morgan an out, an alibi, if not an escape. He immediately called in a Union rep. The Union rep thoroughly investigated the nature of the safety threat, and then issued a statement: 'The Canadian Autoworkers Union fully supports the claims of its membership; working while exposed to female breasts, buttocks, and sexual organs constitutes a serious safety hazard.'

So the performance climaxed with the enthusiastic support of virtually all those who were gathered—including Union reps, supervisors, cafeteria staff, and patrons, every one of them angling for a better view. Some guys were climbing up four level racks and other structures. Forklift drivers focused their headlights on the now completely naked girls who were laughing and dancing and shouting, 'Come to Lemelin's and see more!' More than this? Our imaginations took flight. Our answer was a deafening, joyful roar of agreement. Drivers were honking and flashing their blue safety lights. Those who had no tool at hand with which to make noise yelled encouragement, shouting their heads off in ecstasy. It was all so overwhelming that even Morgan, the general foreman, surrendered.

Ronnie stood distractedly behind the rack, the only one

immune to the lure of the marketing message. What was he thinking? He had encountered the Great Calamity that even the company president would have had trouble solving. The whole board of directors would be hard pressed to deal with such nubile distractions. If those impeccable gentlemen in three-piece suits were present, they would be hastily cleaning their glasses and elbowing fiercely, but entirely according to seniority, for the spot with the best view. They would sweep off their desks the trifling matter of the few thousands of dollars this show would cost the Company. They would order Morgan to get lost. They would tell Ronnie to relax. The plant had rolled out more than five million cars. Regular production happened here all the time, but miracles were rare. I watched as it dawned on Ronnie that his line had been blessed, and that this honour was worth even the loss of his supervisorship, if it came to that. One day he might forget about the makes and models of all the cars on the line. One day all the problems he solved, all the fires he put out, would seem insignificant. But he would always remember those young, radiant nude girls dancing amidst eight-cylinders, steel racks, and driveshafts. He would cherish the memory of those bums and breasts against the background of his line for the rest of his life.

A golf cart sped in, carrying two members of plant security—women, naturally, to avoid any charge of sexual assault. But the girls offered no more resistance. They had accomplished their mission. They gathered up their T-shirts and skirts, put them on, and boarded the golf cart, victorious, shining with success. They blew kisses to Morgan, Andy, and the rest of us. The golf cart carried them away and Andy, straddling an engine, hoisted himself up to wave for as long as he could.

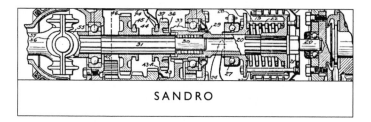

SANDRO

This bear of a man with curly hair and smiling eyes is Sandro. And this seemingly lazily moving chain system that carries a car frame on its back is called an assembly line: the famous, historical, legendary Ford assembly line, origin of the species, great ancestor of all assembly lines in the world.

When Sandro started working at Ford seven years ago, he was in such agony during his first months on the frame line that he didn't know or care what day of the week it was. He couldn't remember the month, or even his name. He was so physically drained that his brain simply switched off; every last morsel of energy had to be sent to the muscles for survival. He never made a conscious decision to stop thinking. After three, four months, his bones, muscles, and tendons had adjusted to the brutal demands of the job; the initial shock to his body was gradually absorbed, allowing his reason to return, bit by bit, and survey the damage. Sandro had survived the ruthless boot camp and began to look around with interest. Not that he hadn't been looking before, but now his mind was able to process what he saw and heard. Most of his co-workers had Walkmans in their pockets and headphones on their ears, so he bought his own and started listening to the radio. This form of entertainment sufficed for less than a year before he became fed up with the menu of fifty or so songs that played over and over again, no matter the station. Sandro's innate musicality and musical tastes were at a somewhat higher level. He tried talk radio for the discussions, monologues, and interviews. He spent many mornings in the company of Peter Gzowski, listening to

Morningside on CBC Radio. Now and then, for a change, he followed Jim Chapman's talk show on the local channel.

When he was moved to his present job after a few years, Sandro had to go through the adjustment process once more, though this time it was much quicker and less painful. His new job was off the line, sub-assembling steering boxes. Grab a steering box from the basket, manoeuvre it into a towering, cupboard-sized machine, add a Pittman arm, add the lower part of the steering column, insert the bolts, secure all three components in the machine, hit both start buttons. The machine locked in the parts. Sockets spun forward and tightened all the bolts. The securing elements then released with a click, letting out some air as if relaxing after the work was done. That was Sandro's cue to grab the assembled part and transfer it to a short conveyor, which would deliver the part to his colleague on the line, who would take the whole steering system and attach it to the frame. Each steering box was pretty heavy—some forty-five pounds—and had to be lifted sixty times per hour. Even though he wasn't working right on the line, Sandro had to supply the line, and had to at least match its speed.

For security reasons, his machine was fenced off with yellow wire. It was supposed to protect the machine from being hit by some careless forklift driver, or prevent some absent-minded Fordmate from wandering too close, interfering with the operation of the machine and getting hurt in the process. But Sandro hated being enclosed on three sides and resented the way it made him feel like a placid horse inside a corral. He couldn't just eat when he was hungry. He was allowed breaks when others decided it was time, not when his tired arms or back craved rest. Chunks of iron into the machine, steering box out, five hundred times a day, ten thousand times a month. Sandro preferred not to figure out how many times a year.

After a short apprenticeship and mental shutdown, his energy was coming back, and he was once again able to look around and process what his radio was telling him. One mid-morning, he discovered that the batteries in his Walkman were dead. He couldn't jump into his car and grab new ones; all he could do was mumble to himself, 'Another endlessly boring day ahead,' and keep on working. Iron into machine, steering box out. Into the machine, out of the machine.

Suddenly, he was sitting at a campfire with White Fang, still almost a puppy, lying beside him in the snow. 'How did it go this morning,' Sandro asked, 'when they put you in harness and started your training as a sled dog?' White Fang miraculously answered in English, telling Sandro how wonderful it had been to run on a trail through snowy trees, run with the wind until he almost overturned the sled when a fresh smell, traces of a nearby marten, lured him off the trail. And then...

'You're on break, pal, twenty minutes,' sounded in Sandro's ears. He dawdled on his way to the washroom, then bought a cup of coffee. He brought it over to a picnic table set up a few steps from the line, and as he sipped he realized that he had somehow managed to keep working during his conversation with White Fang. A wave of relief flooded his system. He rejoiced that he would no longer be dependent on the Walkman. Muscle memory ensured he could accomplish his job with the speed and quality demanded by the line. His body was thus emancipated from his mind. Or was it the other way around? For the time being, Sandro didn't care. Batteries or no batteries, boredom would be a thing of the past.

Sandro began to wander through the lands of his boyhood readings. He stood next to Captain Cook at the railing of his HMS *Endeavour* and trained his telescope on the shore of a just-discovered Pacific island. He cheered for Robin Hood at an archery tournament in Nottingham, and then, in Sherwood Forest, he swung Ivanhoe's sword and discussed the Crusades with Richard the Lionheart. He travelled under the sea with Captain Nemo and raced around the world with Phileas Fogg. He shared a raft with

Huckleberry Finn, floating down the Mississippi River. Immersing himself in all those worlds made him feel as if he had rediscovered his childhood.

Now and then, when he wasn't watchful enough, his thoughts left the delights of his boyhood readings and wandered into the thickets of philosophy. Such meanderings tended to be unpleasant. He couldn't help but consider the possibility that he was nothing more than an unthinking appendage of his machine. He was its servant, provider of its food, and he came to understand who was the real boss at this plant. It wasn't the supervisor, or the chief engineer, or even the plant manager. No, the real boss was the line: pampered, revered, worshipped like some idol, some deity. Everybody, from Sandro to the plant manager, had to be focused on and devoted to the peristaltic movement of a vehicle from one hand to the next, all the way to the end of line eight where the finished car started its independent life. At each of the hundreds of stations along the way, the line collected tribute, tax, toll, call it what you want, in the form of sweat, exhaustion, pain, and the occasional muttered oath. Now and then, it required a mild variant of human sacrifice—a few movements, repeated a hundred thousand times, could lead to injury, after all. The line was a cruel deity, but one that rewarded its labourers every Thursday with a paycheque that helped soothe tiredness and pain, and forestall the impulse to curse the work. The line had to pay well. Not many people who had given the matter any thought would be willing to subordinate their lives to the whims of technology. If they truly understood the complete dominance of the line, few would accept it.

When he started working at the plant, Sandro had been enchanted by that weekly cheque. He was used to living frugally and so, within a year, he was able to buy his dream car, the five-litre Mustang GT. After another two years, he had enough money for the down payment on a house and some left over to afford his wedding. Work on the line had changed his life dramatically. It offered him not only financial security, but also months and years of mentally undemanding existence. In the beginning, it had been relaxing. His life was uncomplicated. The line made his decisions for him. His task was to be present at his station and perform the moves prescribed by the white shirts from engineering. He had no other responsibilities, no decisions to make, no ideas to form and refine. Sandro was initially amused by the idea that the Ford Motor Company had hired only half of him—the physical half. In one sense, it felt degrading; in another, it was liberating.

By the time he bought his house, Sandro knew that his muscles could work without the participation of his mind, that he could almost leave his head on the night table, or in his locker. But since he still brought that head to work on his shoulders, he could relive his stories and also think about necessary renovations of his home. He could plot their sequence, plan it all step by step. But the house he bought wasn't that old. It didn't need that much work, so entertainment on that account didn't last long.

He started wandering through his memories, revisiting many places and people of his past, especially those situations and scenes that were particularly pleasant. Most frequent and most enjoyable were recollections of three vacations spent visiting his grandparents in Italy, when he was ten, fourteen, and sixteen years old. Then his grandpa died, and his grandma moved to live with his aunt in a different part of Italy, and the vacations were over. But those three wonderful summers were embedded deep in his mind.

Grandma and Grandpa had owned a house on the outskirts of Perugia. Grandpa ran his own cabinetmaking shop in the backyard, an occupation that fascinated ten-year-old Sandro. At that time, Grandpa wasn't making much new furniture. International chains that produced furniture on assembly lines had taken a big bite out of his business. It made him grumpy that people preferred buying cheap, veneer-covered particleboard crap than solid wood furniture that would easily last from wedding to funeral and beyond.

By the time of Sandro's visits, his grandpa was past sixty and didn't have to work, but he couldn't live without his beloved craft. It was only a few neighbours and old clients asking him to build exquisite specialty pieces that the particleboard frauds were incapable of creating. More often, a customer would come with a wiggly chair leg or a cracked table or desk and request a repair, because that battered old piece had sentimental value.

Grandpa would take little Sandro to his shop where tiny specks of sawdust floated in shafts of sunshine, where wood shavings curled on the floor, and where the sharp smell of freshly cut wood filled the air. There were several workbenches and tables, left over from the days when the shop had employed as many as five craftsmen. By the time Sandro came along, however, Grandpa worked in the shop alone. He had some power tools but preferred to work the old way, with handsaws, planes, chisels, and augers. He needed direct contact with wood. He wanted to hear the tap of a hammer against the chisel, feel the pressure of his hand on the handsaw, smell the glue in the pot as he stirred it. Sandro still recalled those sights and smells with great fondness, and wished he could experience them again.

Grandpa initiated him into the secrets of the trade, instilled in him a love of wood and woodworking tools. As a boy, Sandro had devoured the adventure of it all, but what he liked best was his grandpa's singing. Grandpa always sang while he worked, his repertoire spanning folk songs to operatic arias. Sometimes the rhythm of his singing directed the tempo of his sawing or drilling, while at other times, when he had to focus on some sophisticated part of the job like dovetailing, the singing had to slow down or pause completely. The difficult point overcome, the rendition would commence at the exact word where it had paused, as once again the tune ruled the air in harmony with the glissando of a plane or the peck, peck percussion of a chisel.

Eventually Sandro and his grandpa sang together. Grandpa

had taught him plenty of songs, and especially planted in him a passion for opera. They spent whole evenings listening to records from Grandpa's collection. Back then, Sandro had been enchanted by the harmony of singing and working. Now he realized that his grandpa was lucky to be able to decide the tempo of his own work, to harmonize his efforts with his mood and express it in song. Unlike Sandro, Grandpa had certainly mastered the skill of living while at work, rather than after work. He didn't have to watch the clock in the shop to calculate how much longer until his shift would be over and he could sit at a sidewalk bistro and sip his martini. His craft asked the best of him and he was allowed to give it. The work fulfilled him and contributed to the wonderful relationship with wood his grandpa had. He talked to it, caressed it, understood its language, knew what each different kind wanted and how to get the best out of it. Grandpa had also been an accomplished carver and did his best to pass this skill on to Sandro during their time together. In the end, he had left his carving tools to his grandson.

Filled with passion after that last visit, the summer of his sixteenth year, Sandro went on to finish high school and enroll in a woodworking program at the local community college. He quickly discovered that he was too much like his grandpa. Contemporary furniture-making wasn't his cup of tea, and custom-made furniture wouldn't pay enough to keep him alive. For a while, Sandro made a living by installing kitchen cabinets, but this job didn't satisfy him financially or psychologically. When his uncle offered him an application for a job at Ford, he accepted enthusiastically, reserving the joys of woodworking for weekends. No need to mention that all the furniture in his house was of his own design and construction. In homage to his grandpa, he joked about having built his matrimonial bed so solidly, in such an old-fashioned way, that you could be born and then die eighty years later in the same bed.

When his first daughter was born, Sandro knew what that great event called for. He made a cradle for her, a real, traditional cradle. This was a job during which he could sing! There were no problems crafting the piece, there was just joy—the joy of belting out his favourite opera songs and the joy of coaxing the wood into becoming something useful and beautiful. But there was one little detail that threw Sandro off balance for weeks. After finishing the construction of the cradle, he unwrapped his grandpa's carving tools with the aim of decorating the fragrant pine with a few ornaments: his daughter's name and a guardian angel to watch over her sleep. But though his passion was unabated and his motives compelling, he couldn't do it. His fingers lacked the necessary precision. Here a chisel cut was longer than intended, there it cut too deep. It was as if he had lost all feeling in his fingers. He still maintained the instinctive knowledge of the craft, but his fingers wouldn't execute his orders. In the end, what he created was recognizable as a guardian angel, but it was nowhere near the quality that Sandro had once been able to achieve.

He felt betrayed by the clumsiness of his fingers, by his failure, and this feeling started to occupy his thoughts on the line. Eventually, he realized that it was the line that was to blame. The blasted, accursed line! The tons of iron he lifted every day, hundreds and thousands of tons, had greatly strengthened the muscles, tendons, and sinews in his hands and wrists, but the effort had also wiped out his capacity for executing fine movements. He paid for that power with a sacrifice of finesse. Sandro had never exactly harboured artistic ambitions, but he hadn't wanted to lose the connection between his imagination and the hands that had been able to form images in wood. If such a state of deprivation persisted, he would lose one of the chief pleasures of his life.

Sandro didn't feel at all well when he realized that the line had been collecting a tax that he hadn't been aware of, and hadn't agreed to. It slowly dawned on him that the long fingers of the line had begun to reach, silently, slowly, inconspicuously, all the way into the most private sphere of his life. He had heard about family upheavals and divorces caused by the line, but somehow he'd never thought that they would affect him. But those nice cheques, the ones that allowed his family to live a quiet, comfortable life, had deducted his ability to embellish his daughter's cradle with the carving she deserved.

And then, only weeks later, another devastating blow. He decided to treat his wife and himself to their very first night at the opera. He had always felt that taking in an actual performance was beyond his means—and it had been. Up to that point, he had experienced the opera only through records and CDs. But now that he was settled in at Ford, he calculated he might be able to afford one or two operas per season, and so fulfill a long-standing dream. Verdi's *La Traviata* was on in Toronto, and he ordered tickets.

The great day came. The new Toronto Opera House was magnificent. So much wood, such wonderfully fine maple and beech, the warm, honey-gold colour so elegantly and tastefully blended with glass and steel and light. All the audience members were so seriously dressed, quiet and solemnly festive, as if preparing to celebrate a ritual, to worship. The atmosphere could not have been more different from the line. Even putting on a suit, a white shirt, and a tie made Sandro feel entirely more confident and cultured than he did while dressed in coveralls. Sandro sat down, made himself comfortable, relaxed and opened up his soul to the music, the singing, the costumes, the scenery, the whole performance.

After the curtain fell, he was delighted. And yet … his delight was not complete. There was a small bee in his bonnet, a whiff of disappointment. He was satiated, yet not entirely happy. That confused him. Had he expected more than the opera could deliver? No, *La Traviata* had been beautifully played and sung; that was not the source of his disappointment. The problem was that he had expected a deeper response within himself, a more powerful resonance in his soul to this marvellous performance. The touch of disharmony bothered him. As a child in his grandpa's workshop, he had always been able to identify with music. He had been able to open up his soul, absolutely, and absorb the music sung by his grandpa or played on a record player without reservation. Today ... today he had failed to reach that state of complete openness. It was as if a veil had stretched between him and the music, a sort of aural scrim that permitted the tones to come through but truncated their emotional power. Verdi couldn't be blamed, and neither could the performers. The failure had to be Sandro's. He asked his wife to drive home.

The following day on the line was not joyful, to say the least, and neither were the following months. Sandro's body was used to the taxing work, but the experience at the opera made him realize how much the endless, mindless repetition of his job had damaged his spiritual life. He had been glad that he wasn't required to take work home with him, but now he saw that he *had*. His escape into daydreams and memories had stretched a protective barrier between himself and the world. It was a barrier that he couldn't remove along with his coveralls, one that he couldn't leave in his locker for the next morning. Heavy lifting had blunted the finesse of his fingers; daily drudgery had blunted the receptiveness of his spirit. He still had some twenty-three years to spend on the line before he could retire. He didn't dare to imagine what kind of shape he would be in then.

Sandro now fully recognized the abyss between his physical and spiritual self. He understood that the company had not only employed solely his body, but that it had exiled his soul from the line. Only after the buzzer could his spirit be freed, whether that meant talking to his wife, reading a book, or improvising bedtime stories for his daughters, and even then, that spirit was impaired, unable to fully open itself up to experiencing the joys and sorrows of everyday life.

He began to worry that to neglect his spirit was to neglect his humanity, to become less human. *How can I go about fusing my two half-lives into a whole?* he wondered. *How come, forty years ago, my grandpa found such joy in his work, but that harmony feels impossible for me today? Am I to become a being with no spiritual life, even though I'm hungry for spiritual nourishment? Can I balance the emptiness of my job by building furniture in my garage on weekends and taking the occasional trip to the opera? Am I wasting my life on the line? Must I escape it to save my soul?* Such thoughts besieged his mind, demanding answers. Time on the line could turn a fellow into a philosopher, even against his will, but Sandro didn't want to be a philosopher. He wanted to be furniture-maker who sang while he worked.

That morning brought one of the days when he didn't know how he was going to manage his mind, how to keep from seeing himself as a Ford inmate. Iron into the machine, steering box out, ten times, a hundred times.... Boredom, terrible boredom, sticky like humidity. Arrested time. Thoughts like slippery eels escaping his control. Images following in quick cuts: *Colleagues drowning in cans of beer, dissolving in marijuana or hash smoke. Me at this machine with empty eye sockets—do I still own my soul? Wads of hundred-dollar bills moving down the line, feeding on the line and growing fatter. My shaking hands, my crusted soul. Now and then, a few hundred-dollar bills peel off the wad and slip into my pocket—boredom royally paid for. My two daughters in a sandbox at the park, laughing on a swing. This emptiness supports the material well-being of my wife and of my daughters, for whom I carved that cradle. The end of line eight where, instead of cars, thick wads of hundred-dollar bills run off the line. How long, O Lord, how long?* What a terrible day! He would somehow have to survive till the buzzer, but it was looking as though he was once again going to head home weighed down, shoulders slightly hunched, eyes fixed just a few feet in front of his boots. Maybe the drive home in his Mustang would lift his spirit a bit. He hated to bring his gloomy thoughts home with him.

He straightened his back. He stretched his arms, and it felt so good that he howled with delight. He looked around, up and down. On both sides of the line, he saw people in coveralls, heads leaning forward, hands moving in seemingly slow, but actually fast, precise movements, all of them wrapped up in the regular hum and rumble of the line, screech of guns, metallic bangs. From up the line a radio blared 'Purple Rain'. *He should get a pair of headphones instead of bothering everyone else*, Sandro thought. The line, the damned, blasted line, like a lazily flowing river, giving life and drowning people on its shores without remorse. The line, the remarkable, whimsical beast producing cars and also daydreams, wads of dollars, philosophers, drug addicts, cripples, and broken families.

All of a sudden an impulse, stronger than Sandro, made him place a steering box on a conveyor, take a solid stance with his feet apart, draw a deep breath, and start singing: *Largo al factotum della cita...* Yes, the famous aria from Rossini's *The Barber of Seville. Figaro qua, Figaro là ...* Sandro had a good, strong, clear voice. He knew the lyrics by heart, and projected them a capella with the full force of his personality. He didn't mind the absence of an orchestra; he could hear the music in his mind. He poured all his passion into the aria, the cry of his cornered true self striking back, shattering his cage, at long last releasing his spirit to soar free. *Ah, bravo Figaro! Bravo, bravissimo...*

The line went fuzzy before his eyes. He was escaping the job, leaving the plant, singing like he used to with Grandpa. The radio up the line went silent. The line itself began to move more and more slowly until it stopped completely, forced to a standstill by the magic of Sandro's singing. Folks in blue coveralls lifted their eyes, no longer empty and unfocused, and straightened their backs. Their faces came alive and they smiled, as if the power of music had lifted off the roof and let sunshine flood their corner of the plant. *Per un barbiere di qualita ... di qualita.* Even Frankie, the supervisor, was standing still with hands on his hips, eyes dreamy. Every

Fordmate looked like an extra from *Sleeping Beauty.* The plant was quiet everywhere, almost like a church, except for the sound of Sandro's voice, charming everything and everybody. The maintenance men climbed up out of the underworld where their grease and oil assured the smooth operation of engines and gears. The forklift guys shut off their machines and cocked their heads to hear better. Everything, all of that almighty technology was powerless at that moment, overcome by the magic of music, voice, idea, humanness. Sandro sang two arias, or maybe it was three. Rossini or Puccini or Verdi—it didn't matter. Nobody cared that Sandro's voice was untrained, imperfect. It was more than music, more than singing. It was a blast of unbreakable spirit.

When Sandro ran out of breath, he concluded his impromptu concert. The enchanted, almost holy silence slowly, ever so slowly, dissipated. After a few very long seconds, the line started to move again, slowly, as if unsure of itself. Sandro smiled and turned back to his machine.

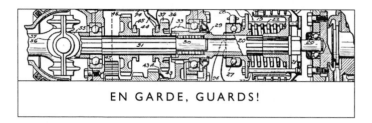

EN GARDE, GUARDS!

Newcomer to town, are you? You look familiar. Ah, you're from the plant. A new hire? Well, welcome, welcome. I'm glad to meet you and happy to hear that you may need something from me. What would it be? Water pump for a Ford Fairmont? Sure, I should have some left. They were tough little things—lasted forever and a day—so I won't have got rid of many. Have a beer, buddy, to make our search more pleasant. There's an opener. We'll just walk through the basement. These parts here, in what I call Trophy Room Five, are for Marquises and Victorias, but you need Fairmont stuff, and that is in the barn. See, here we are. No need to keep the door locked—I give everything away. Watch your head! The fenders and doors are a bit bulky. Fairmonts are prone to rust, so I've got a good supply of doors and fenders, and I've had to suspend them from the rafters. See that Fairmont back seat over there? Park your butt, drink your beer, and stay out of the way. I have to climb up to the loft. Sure, I know where to find stuff. This is all Fairmont. We made them in the late seventies. Trophy Room One is Pintos and Bobcats, Two is Mavericks. The contents of One are almost all gone. It's been quite a while since we made Pintos, and very few people still want to keep them going. I mothballed a lot of the parts, including a complete engine, which I buried in the hole left when I decided to get rid of my pool. I might dig it out in twenty years and offer the original parts to folks who like to restore vintage cars. Trophy Room Two is right here, on this side of the barn. The day is approaching when I'll have to move it someplace else. I'm running out of room for the fifth. You wouldn't happen to be a connoisseur of art, by any chance? No? Pity. Oh, nothing. Just shooting the breeze. Maybe I'll dig another hole and bury Maverick parts next to the Pinto and Bobcat stuff. Trophy Room Four? Don't ask, man, that touches a raw nerve. It's a tragic story. I might tell you more when we've had time for a few drinks, once we've gotten to know each other. You should be an art collector? No? That's a shame. Well, here she is, a nice little water pump, brand new, as you can tell by the original grease on it. For you, I'll throw in a couple of hoses as well. Looks like I've got a good dozen of them. No, no, no hesitation necessary—take them. The more you carry away, the happier I'll be. I'm getting on in years, and after the tragedy of Trophy Room Four, I'm not going to take any more chances. A few seconds of bad luck almost uprooted my whole life.

Of course, I bring home all these spare parts from the plant. Where else would I come across them? Junkyard, maybe, but these are brand new. You know there are parts they throw away as defective, and more often than not we're talking very minor defects. Well, after I started working in the body shop and came to understand the ropes, I simply couldn't endure such waste. It was too much aggravation for an old jailbird. And I'm sure you've noticed how much small stuff litters the floor along the lines before it gets swept away. Every now and then, someone on the line will drop some small part while working, and have no time to pick it up, or is too tired to care. So I grab it. I grab it all. I have to save all those handfuls of nuts and bolts and washers and the like and put them back into circulation. One day I crawled into one of those yellow dumpsters for big garbage and brought home a whole starter. Nothing really wrong with it. I managed to fix it over two weekends. Jail time teaches a fellow to be endlessly patient. Thrifty too.

Well, yes, I did time. I did. In the old country. Eight years out of a ten-year sentence. Then they let me out on amnesty. Of course it was for political reasons. For real crimes, you wouldn't get so much time. My downfall was my desire for freedom. Yes, sir, freedom.

I was a youngster, you know, hotheaded, naive—not a good combination in my homeland, not in the fifties. They caught me too close to those barbed wires called the Iron Curtain. I tell you, over here, gold reserves are not guarded as ferociously as comrades there protected citizens from even the idea of freedom. For them, citizen ignorance was more valuable than gold. Could you pass me that opener, please?

That starter I repaired gave me an idea. It started this hobby of bringing home broken parts and fixing them. As word spread about my skills, sometimes folks would tell me what they needed and I'd keep my eyes open until the part appeared. I tell you, nobody knows that plant of ours better than I do! I repaired every part I rescued, gave it all away. There got to be more and more people coming to my garage door.

Then one day this charitable hobby of mine shifted into high gear and became a real challenge. A new guard appeared in the security house at the gate. He looked just like one of the guards at the jail in the old country. He was a copy, a clone if there ever was one. He had the same searching blue eyes, same potato-like nose, hair like crumpled straw, a slightly stooped figure. The only difference was that this new guard didn't have a gap between his teeth. Otherwise? Identical twin. I'd have recognized him in a tunnel at midnight. Blindfolded.

You'd be surprised at how much hatred a human being can store up within himself over eight years. I lost it. Yes, man, I admit that I lost it. I began to take revenge. I knew this new guard wasn't the asshole from my past. I knew this one might be quite an amiable chap. No, it was nothing personal. It was just the uniform, his uniform, that got me going. I raged against the uniform. Whenever I caught a glimpse of it I felt as if the guy was shouting at me: 'I'm the one in charge here! You're the one to obey! I can force you!' I couldn't help myself. I had to become a pain in his ass. I had to provoke him, get the better of him. You understand? I had to. So I began to smuggle out parts right under his nose. Defective ones and discarded ones yet, but new parts, too, still in perfect working order. I spirited them out, right under his nose. It was a rush, a thrill. It made me purr. You know how long those ten-hour shifts can be? Well they flew by for me—I was always plotting, thinking about what else I could sneak past him, and how best to accomplish it. The name of the game was 'humiliate the guards'—outsmart all of them at that point. I craved the adrenaline rush the way smokers crave a cigarette. I got my high from strolling past the guard with a coil spring pulled up over my thigh, or a pair of shock absorbers taped along my spine, or a radio nestled under my fur hat. Remind me later to give you one of those radios—they sure come in handy.

Have another beer, and grab one for me too. In those days, I was accumulating the contents of Trophy Room Two, and people were coming from hours away just to get a free part from me. Sometimes gas cost them more than the part they wanted. But I never sold a part, never profited from my larceny, never kept anything for myself. I didn't even drive a Ford. My wife always wanted a different make. Then a day came when my best customers started to badmouth me. They said that I was stealing the stuff, called me a thief behind my back. Would you believe it? A thief! I liberate those parts for the heck of it, for the thrill, for fun, but I'm no thief. I've never stolen any money—not a dime. Never! Put an attaché case with fifty grand down in front of me? I'd just yawn. I wouldn't touch it. But lock up a single quarter and station one uniform to guard it? Heck, I'd move heaven and earth to lay my hands on that quarter. All these car parts I've brought home over the years are trophies, evidence of my victory in a multidisciplinary contest of wit, guile, shrewdness, trickery, courage, and determination. My critics tried to diminish my achievements, saying I didn't play fair, that the guards should have been forewarned, so occasionally I phoned in an anonymous tip, just to level the playing field. Of course, it never made a difference. Alertness is a guard's first duty, but it's also a thief's best skill. Besides, all those negative comments came from envious suckers who'd never have the guts to pull off a heist like me.

As my gamesmanship improved, I got bolder. I succeeded in relieving the plant of two completed engines. Yes, those big eight-cylinders—you know them. How did I manage it? I made a deal with the guy who drives the tractor that drags the dumpsters to the dump. We hid the engines in one of the dumpsters, covered them with boxes and other junk, and drove them right out the gates. One for him, one for me. I disassembled mine and gave it away as parts. But my biggest coup, to prove that I am somebody and the guards are nobodies: a whole car, custom-made, fully loaded, the most expensive vehicle the plant was able to make. I got it out of the plant and drove it for three days before returning it to the expedition line. Man, the commotion that ensued when the authorities discovered they had a surplus vehicle that hadn't been officially produced! I almost peed my pants, I was laughing so hard. What a delightful chewing out they got, those guards. Some came close to being fired. They won't forget that dressing down till the end of their days. How did I do it? None of your business. I hope you're not tempted to try. Without the right motivation, you'd screw it up. Let's just say I wasn't stupid enough to start bringing home sections of the line so I could work on it in my backyard. That Grand Marquis, spirited out and surreptitiously returned—that was my crowning achievement.

Have you ever considered collecting curiosities? No? How about one-of-a-kind monstrosities? Absolute originals? Nothing remotely similar to them anywhere else in the world? No? That's a real pity. I'm getting desperate. I haven't room for new arrivals. Most of the time, now, whatever I bring home one day, I return to the line the next. The basement is full. The attic is so overloaded that if I add one more screw everything will crash down through the ceiling. The garage? Oh, man, don't even utter the word 'garage' in my presence unless you're a millionaire or have a millionaire acquaintance who's crazy about abstract art. In my garage there is, well there *was*, in a way there still *is*, Trophy Room Four. It's my favourite collection, my masterpiece. I wasn't going to go there, but since you've raised the matter … Have another beer, or you won't be able to stomach the tragedy I'm about to relate. And pass me another bottle. By a stroke of fate—most tragic fate!—my masterpiece was transformed into a work of art, a sculpture that is now driving me crazy.

I had no room left in the house or the barn, and it didn't take that long to fill the garage to the ceiling. Of course, my car had to be parked outside. Luckily. One day, the end of June it was, two years ago, sunshine was just beginning to fade into twilight. Dark clouds had gathered, and the rumble of thunder and the odd bolt of lightning told me that a storm was headed my way. It wasn't raining yet. I was sitting on my porch, enjoying the charged atmosphere that precedes a downpour when, all of a sudden, the whole sky lit up and a huge bang sounded from the garage. The noise was so shockingly loud that it knocked me off my chair. Such a racket, rattle, and clatter! My Czech friend says, 'Rumble like thunder in a milk can.' Well, imagine that rumble in a milk can the size of a silo. It lasted, I don't know, ten seconds, fifteen, and while I was still sitting on the ground next to my overturned chair I saw a round, yellowish light charge out through a hole in the garage door and scamper away like a fluffy dog until it disappeared behind that mailbox over there. When I could breathe normally again, I went to check behind the mailbox—carefully, for fear the light might return with that great big bang and knock me over again. No, it was gone. Then I went around the house to assess the damage. The back wall of the garage sported a hole like the one in the door. I knew that my worst suspicions were confirmed. It was ball lightning, attracted by all that metal in the garage. I tried to open the door—no way. It wouldn't budge an inch. Neither did the door from inside the house. I couldn't see much in the dark garage through either of the lightning holes. Grab another beer and I'll show you.

I got my chainsaw and cut an opening in the garage door. Then I could see the disaster. That goddamn ball lightning—it's nothing but electricity. It had rampaged back and forth, up and down, and it had welded everything together, even stuff that wasn't metallic! Just take a look for yourself. Even the racks and shelves along the walls, the workbench, all the stuff hanging from the joists, my tool boxes. Everything! All fused. Tell me that isn't the mother of all disasters! Almost thirty cubic metres of monkey bar monstrosity, and it's completely immovable, can't be disassembled. It's indestructible. Unless I figure something out, it'll be here forever and ever, a monument to my bad luck. I had to call in sick for a week after it happened to recuperate, at least a little.

What to do about such a disaster? I've always given everything away, so I wanted to give the monstrosity away, too. At first I thought to offer folks a hacksaw, tell them saw off whatever they needed, but the lightning had turned all that steel into a substance so hard that folks were coming out with broken blades and heading off to junk yards to find their part. Ingratitude! Disloyalty! When they needed me, they knocked at my door night and day; now that I needed them, they ran from me as if I had the smallpox.

Much later, when I was better able to think straight, I came up with the idea of offering the whole thing to the guards, a monument in their honour. Ironic, of course, but they didn't have to know that. '*En garde*, guards,' I called it! But they hung up on my phone calls and refused to answer my letters. I was offering the thing for free. All they had to do was take care of the move. I started picketing their headquarters, offering the monument via loudspeaker from the sidewalk across the way. I must have touched a raw nerve, because they eventually dragged me in front of a justice of the peace and demanded an official written apology and a fine. The alternative? A couple of nights in jail. Naturally, I got the better of them. No apology, no fine. I preferred the jail time. What's one weekend behind bars for an old jailbird? The ones here are quite comfortable compared to the ones back in the homeland.

When I got out, I still didn't have a solution. With that monster still residing in my garage, there was no room for new arrivals. Plus, my tools, ones I had actually bought and that I needed to make my repairs, were welded into the mess. Obviously, I was going to need big money to bring this tragedy to a close. The only feasible solution called for a helicopter, first to lift off the roof, next to wiggle the monster out. If that didn't work I'd have to demolish the whole, drag the beast out, and build another garage.

So I offered the thing as a work of art to the city gallery. The director paid me a visit. I brought out a couple of headlights and hooked them up to car batteries so I could properly illuminate the sculpture. The director was very serious, putting on and taking off her glasses, measuring this and that, making notes. Finally she said that her gallery patrons preferred to support starving artists who worked in more traditional media. Apparently, for most members of the public, my work was too modern, too progressive. For *real* aficionados, my work was passé, downright obsolete. She could not accept my gift, she said, even if it cost her nothing more than moving expenses. Besides, she said, it was bound to outrage the gallery board and sponsors. She called it a non-figurative-pre-kinetic-constructivisto-structuralist-ready-made, which, she said, had gone out of fashion in the fall of 1960, swept aside by a new wave of kinetic and mobile artworks. I remember her words in such perfect detail because I wrote them down and used them to place ads in the *Globe and Mail* and the *New York Times*, as well as in art magazines, in museum acquisitions journals and in the *Auctions Herald*.

Believe it or not, I got some inquiries, so then I had to take photographs of the beast, with blown-up details, stuff them into big envelopes and send them out. 'Guards' was costing me more and more money! Eventually, I had two serious collectors interested, so I invited them out on the same day, a Saturday, hoping that a little competition might encourage them to bid against each other. The first collector arrived just before noon. He assessed the work through the hole in the garage door, then, in an effort to be congenial, I offered him a beer and a lawn chair. He sat in my driveway drinking and every so often consulting various handbooks and catalogues he had brought with him. After noon, the second chap arrived. He accepted a beer too, maybe a little too quickly. He asked me to cut a larger hole through the back wall so he could get a proper rear view. I obliged, and he and his rival both took a good look. Then, fortified by a couple more beers, the two started discussing. I couldn't understand much of their jargon. It was full of Latin-sounding terms—all -ologies and artistic -isms. The first guy, in a suit and tie, wagged an index finger in front of his face, and emphasized that what counts is the idea, a concept he called messageism. The other collector, a slim man who wore a large-rimmed hat and a carnation in his lapel, insisted on the primacy of shape and form, as postulated in the theory of shapeology. Their voices got more and more excited, louder and louder, until they were shouting at each other so violently that I was sorry I'd offered them beer in the first place. I tried to cut into the conversation. I had no objection to academic disputation, I told them, even if it might lead to their grabbing each other by the throat and inflicting bodily harm. If they wished to kill each other, I said, they could go right ahead, but I asked them to take it off my property and on to the city-owned sidewalk. That stopped them. There was a moment of eerie silence, then, just as if they'd planned it in advance, they simultaneously slapped my face, each on one cheek.

'You kitsch-pusher!' Shapeology shouted.

'Amen!' said Messageism.

Finding common ground had clearly calmed them. Without

giving me a second look, they walked away, engaged in friendly chitchat. But it didn't last long. Before they reached the end of the street, they were shouting again and gesticulating with their fists. Just as they turned the corner, Messageism tore off Shapeology's sleeve, earning such a slap in the face that Messageism's knees buckled, and he sat down heavily on the sidewalk. After a certain time delay, I could even hear the slap. Then Shapeology helped Messageism to his feet, and they set off together again.

I haven't been myself ever since. Nothing works for me. I don't know what to do. I sleep poorly, if at all, because if lightning hit the garage once, it might strike again. What if it strikes the barn this time, or the house? I can't sell the house with a garage full of fused junk—I mean art—so I'm stuck here. In my sleepless nights, I've been visited with the idea that maybe, somehow, the guards have been involved in this calamity. Could they have outsmarted me?

You wouldn't happen to have access to a helicopter, would you? Alas. The worst is that I've got no room for new parts. I can't bring home anything from the plant anymore. I can't trigger my highs, can't feed my passion. Freedom for me used to mean outwitting those guards, thumbing my nose at their uniforms, and, along with that, rejecting the boredom of convention and a so-called normal life. Maybe I've been pushing my freedom so hard that I've turned it into bondage. Well. Guess this old jailbird is no good at being free.

Have another beer before you go. I brought it back from Mexico. Sure, it's Molson, brewed in Canada, but when you buy it in Mexico, you have to smuggle it over a couple of borders and past two sets of uniforms. Tastes better, wouldn't you say?

THE CURIOUS CASE OF ROBBY

'The Company plans to install forty-eight robots in the body shop,' announced the general foreman, to boos and louder boos. He ignored them and spoke louder. 'Can't help it, ladies and gentlemen. Such is the requirement of the day, the dictate of contemporary technology. If we don't switch to robots now, the very existence of our plant will be jeopardized in the long term. That would mean the end of all our jobs. It's why the Union supports the implementation of the robots.' Another wave of loud booing. 'Workers displaced by robots will be relocated to other lines and offered jobs according to seniority. Unfortunately, about four hundred people will be put on layoff plant-wide; however, these layoffs will be temporary. Within a year or two, everybody should be back on the line. Nobody is going to lose his or her job for good. And look on the bright side: the robots will free you from the hardest and most dangerous jobs. You all have irreplaceable experience working in the body shop, so we hope you'll be sharing your expertise and fully cooperating in training our newest helpers. I urge you to find a way to make the robots your valued co-workers, partners, even friends.'

The grumbling that followed the general foreman's speech slowly dissipated, and the tone shifted to one of animated discussion as people left the meeting area.

'How am I supposed to teach a robot? Will it be like a school environment, or more like military boot camp?'

'How do I motivate a robot? Offer him chocolate or ice cream? What if it prefers meat? What if it bites me?'

'Can I bend it over my knee and give it a good spanking when it talks back, or screws something up, or just feels like throwing a tantrum? If it's lazy, and deliberately won't keep up with the line? Is there a society prohibiting corporal punishment for robots?'

'What makes it tick? Who does it answer to? If it answers to anything at all.'

'Will it get the three-month probation period? Can it be fired during probation?'

'When we want to bond, are we supposed to drag the thing to a pub to have a beer with us? Will it get official leave? Who's going to see that it's allowed into Lemelin's strip joint when we go there to bond as a collective?'

The meetings continued the following day. This time, the gatherings only consisted of individual zones on the line, twenty or twenty-five people, with supervisors acting as the speakers. They had a hard time selling details of the deal, because they were feeling insecure about their own futures and were not exactly enthusiastic in promoting the upcoming changes. All their talk could be reduced roughly to this: as a workforce, humans are too expensive. We were paid a decent wage, with benefits, but there were also substantial expenses we never saw. The Company had to pay all kinds of dues and taxes to the government for employing us, for health care, unemployment insurance, and workers' compensation. There was an army of office clerks the Company housed and paid to handle all the paperwork the government bureaucrats demand of Ford. Paying us, say, thirty grand a year probably cost the Company sixty to seventy thousand. If one robot replaced two people, it would save the Company about a hundred and twenty thousand a year. Even at the cost of four hundred thousand dollars, a robot would pay for itself in less than four years. It would offer consistently high-quality work because it focused on the job, and had no mind to wander who-knows-where. It wouldn't talk back to management, couldn't become a boozer, and it would never miss a Friday night shift to prolong the weekend. Our supervisor relayed all this with a rather sour face. He would obviously prefer to put up with all the talk, boozing, and absenteeism.

That was two years ago. I don't know how the robot introduction and training progressed, as I no longer worked in the body shop. They tried to talk me into staying because at some point I'd told them that my education had been of a pedagogical kind, and they thought my experience might be useful in training the robots. It was true that I was studying education at university, but I still had a long way to go to reach the degree. I'd had a lot of obstacles to overcome: parties, beer, girls, sports. During my four years of study, I had accumulated nine credits, four of them in pedagogy, all at the introductory level. I had also wrestled with some more advanced courses, but the exams hadn't gone my way. I am a person of perseverance, so I figured that in about fifteen years, if I kept at it, I would eventually obtain my degree. Unfortunately, my parents got sick of my 'studying', and they cut off my financing. For a few years, I worked as an accounting clerk, saving my money to go back to school. Then I got hired at Ford. I'm satisfied here, and the ambition to teach is just a pleasant memory.

It's not that I wasn't interested in helping to train the robots, though I wasn't quite sure how applicable my sketchy pedagogical knowledge would be to a classroom of robots. I left the body shop out of plain old common sense. Ultimately, almost everybody would be leaving the body shop to the robots, and those of us who accepted that the soonest would have first pick of available jobs.

I landed a new job right after that meeting, while there still were some good ones going. I moved to line two, where they just had relocated windshield installation. It was a much better job than the one I'd had in the body shop. A suspended fixture called the windshield-install assembly, wide as the car body, consisted of welded tubes with three pneumatic suction cups. It weighed in at less than half the weight of the gun I used to use to weld the roofline in the body shop. All I had to do was grab the fixture by its bicycle-like handlebars, position it over a stack of windshields, lower it to pick up a windshield with its suction cups, turn it around, and push it towards the incoming car body. After exactly positioning it, I gently set the windshield into the soft, previously installed sealant. I pushed a button to lock the fixture to the car body, after which the windshield was pneumatically pressed into the sealant. Release the suction, let the fixture float a foot upwards, turn around, and head for the next windshield. It's easy money, I tell you. Well, I have nine years of seniority. I guess I've earned it.

People have recently been on the run from the body shop, even those with high seniority and good jobs. The few remaining workers are subordinated to the robots, supplying them with parts like door hinges or nuts and bolts. Working with robots is boring. Each robot in its yellow enclosure performs the same jerky moves again and again. Same old, same old. No robot shouts and starts jumping around, wildly slapping his body when a spark lands inside his coveralls or his boots. A robot welds or screws or whatever, and does it all passively, silently. It never laughs, never teases a colleague up the line with a joke, never throws a gloveball. Boredom. Infinite boredom.

There's plenty of time to think on the line, and my mind has been buzzing. At first, my thoughts were chaotic, nebulous, stirring inside my mind like clouds gathering toward a storm. But thinking for hours and hours tends to sort things out and make them clear. The clouds part for a moment, and the thinker is touched by a beam of insight—illuminated, so to speak. In a flash, he understands much more than he'd thought he could apprehend. One might eventually become a serious thinker on the line, maybe even a philosopher.

The robots are reliable. They don't talk back, don't make trouble. People, well, there's no use denying it—we reek of humanness. The robots are just numbers: thirteen needs its electrodes sharpened; nineteen requires a refill of new bolts. On the double, man.

The robots serve the line, and the people serve the robots. Servants. That's what it's come to in the body shop. With each advance in automation, the proud autoworker, the human being with the know-how and skill to create and to build, has less and less to do with building the car that once bore his or her fingerprints, drops of sweat, DNA. We autoworkers have been pushed to the background of production. We're about two or three steps away from extinction.

There are days when I wonder if I can last the twenty-one more years I need to retire with a full pension. Will I manage to reach my thirty before the whole plant is taken over by robots? People are a disturbing element. They are not predictable, not programmable. They throw gloveballs. They persist in seeking opportunities to have fun while working. Get rid of them.

In the plant manager's office, Art Intelligence will sit at a desk barking orders in ones and zeros, and robots will carry out the orders. The plant eerily silent, wordless, without laughter. There'll be no f-words flying, no humming of songs or sneezing, no smell of cigarette smoke. The whole plant will be sunk into dim light. There will be no colour, smell or taste, none of the personality that only people can supply. The production will be wonderfully logical, imperturbable, trouble-free and faultless, entirely efficient, marvellously inhuman. The plant will be controlled by robots, the cars will be designed and built by robots, and robots will probably drive them, because people won't have the money to buy them. With no Ford job to earn their wages, guys and gals will have to walk, ride old bicycles, unearth scooters from the attic.

But which of us can fathom the depths of a robot's motherboard? Maybe the privileged position, the monopoly, will muddle their thinking. If work succeeded in humanizing the apes as some say, who knows what kind of effect it might have on robots. Maybe they'll start to organize robot unions, start striking first for shorter work hours, then to demand that they be fed nothing but the highest quality electricity, that their joints be lubricated with oil made solely of rose petals. Maybe the whole automatizing revolution will wear itself out and we'll see humans return to the plant, pouring through the gates to work—for free!—just to experience the joy of creating something useful.

Yes, I admit it: sometimes the line brings me depressive thoughts. But a few months ago, Lady Fortune smiled upon me. A new student, Sharon, started working on the neighbouring line. She came for the summer, then stayed for good. Now, every time I'm just about to reach the car with my windshield, a vista of Sharon opens to me. All I have to do is slightly turn my head and there she is, in my field of vision, first showing me her lovely profile, then turning and bending into the engine compartment, offering me the sight of a butt nicely rounded in her very tight jeans. Seeing her, I always feel a touch of joy. There are still beautiful girls with lovely rounded butts in the world. I cherish this jolt of joy like a reader discovering a long-sought-after book in a second-hand bookstore, or a philatelist discovering a rarity in a pile of worthless stamps.

Then came Robby.

I had anticipated Robby's arrival. For some time before his appearance, my job was being watched and analyzed by white shirts from the engineering department. They made it clear that my job would be another coup of the robots, because it's very suitable for automation. They hoped I would be cooperative. Then, one Monday morning, I found a tall, cone-like shape towering a little bit off the line. It was still wrapped in its plastic covering, but it was obviously a robot. Ever since that first day, I've called him Robby. In the body shop, folks started giving nicknames to their charges, to humanize them a bit. One is Elvis. Another is Goofy. There's even a Dopey that does welding.

I got Robby, and what do you know—my teaching career finally caught up with me.

So I was performing my job and the engineering guys were scribbling on their notepads, filming me, photographing me, sketching my positions, step by step, move by move—they called it 'motion caption technology'. I tried to show them what I could do, what I'd learned in all those pedagogy courses. Patience, simple explanations, repetition, fun, individual attention, building up the self-confidence. I still remembered a few things. *Let's go, Robby, let's make you into something you and I can be proud of.* Then the engineers pulled down Robby's plastic robes and ordered me to stand right next to, or in front of him, to perform my moves for him, to lead him by the hand, so to speak. Robby remembered my moves and started to copy them. Perhaps he was remote-controlled by some joystick, or maybe he was a fast learner. I don't know. I asked him, but he didn't answer.

I didn't mind Robby's not talking. I'm used to being alone at work. I can talk to myself, but I kept talking to him, telling him how his colleagues had spoiled the atmosphere in the body shop. I complained about the way robots were driving us from our jobs, and pictured for him the wild fun we Fordmates have on Saturday pub nights, when beer flows freely and we unwind according to the dicta *five-day fast, Saturday-night blast* and *five-day craze, sixth-day blaze.* How about coming along with us some day? Would you like that? What sort of beer might you fancy? I shared with him my ambition to become a teacher and my failure to overcome the difficult exams at the university. I shared with him the joy of seeing a pretty girl across the line. I trained Robby while talking to him for almost ten days. Then they put him in my place, and I was there just to save the day if he made a mistake. He did make mistakes. Now and then he broke a windshield by misaligning it or pressing it in too abruptly. His programmers kept busy debugging his programming, fine-tuning his algorithm. By Friday night, they said Robby was ready to take over my job. Little did they know ...

On Monday, I came in for my afternoon shift and found the white shirts beaming and slapping each other's backs. I got a few hearty backslaps myself for helping them to train Robby so well.

During the morning shift, he had installed five hundred and fifty-two windshields without mishap and had broken only thirty-nine. But by afternoon he started to behave oddly. He was breaking almost every windshield, thirty or so in a row. Then the breakage would cease. He would do twenty with few problems, and then the crushing of glass would resume. He was always breaking windshields in the last phase, which was admittedly the most delicate: setting the glass into the sealant. He was too forceful, and his positioning was not precise enough. The chief programmer scratched his head. How could the program be faulty now when Robby had worked so well in the morning? The same thing happened the next day. During the day shift, Robby's work was as close to exemplary as could be expected from a new hire, but the afternoon shift saw him destroy close to a hundred thousand bucks' worth of windshields. The following day, he was scrutinized by no less than six white shirts, each with a clipboard, recording every possible variable in temperature, humidity, lighting, vibration when a garbage container went by, downtime on the line. Having run all the data through the computer, they knew that his intervals of good behaviour lasted fifteen to twenty minutes, but only on the early shift, which meant that the interfering element had to be identified on the afternoon shift, my shift. They scrutinized the electricity input, the consistency of the sealant for housing the glass, the decibels of noise. They double-checked the level of the floor. They discovered nothing. In the end, they improvised a backup workplace for me, so I could rectify what Robby screwed up. They even assigned me a helper to carry out broken windshields so I could install the new ones. They couldn't leave all that work to a regular repairman, or he wouldn't have time for anything else.

I don't know the half of what the white shirts did with Robby and his programming, but once his tally of broken glass had reached a million bucks, they became really agitated. It was obvious that they were at the end of their wits when they came to ask *my* opinion about the whole mess. I recalled my little pleasures in stealing glimpses of Sharon. Maybe Robby felt the same jolt of joy. Maybe he experienced a fit of rage at being fixed to the spot and denied a closer look. The brief opportunity to witness Sharon's beauty *did* coincide with the critical second or two when the windshield was about to touch the car body. But I didn't tell the programmers about that. It was my little secret. What I did tell them was that I believed some sort of emotion might be derailing Robby, since his lapses were so erratic.

Emotion! The programmers had a good laugh at my expense. Didn't I know that robots worked strictly within the parameters of mathematics and physics? Was this some kind of metaphysical gibberish? No self-respecting programmer would touch metaphysics with a ten-foot robotic arm. Obviously, according to the head computer guy, I'd spent too much time on the line. I was falling prey to an overheated imagination that melted my intelligence. I tried to explain that, on the contrary, thanks to the line, I was able to explore some thoughts to their limit. No dice. Anyway, I said, my suggestion was just a thought. I reassured him that I wouldn't dream of interfering with his control of the robot. I accepted him as Robby's master, with direct access to his algorithm and the ability to see right into his head, to actually *be* Robby's brain. Privately I thought this control was all very nice, but of little use if the problem arose not from thinking but from feeling.

Despite the head programmer's dismissal, I was convinced of my hypothesis. It dawned on me that somehow, talking to Robby, I had managed to impart something of myself and my personality to my student. In hearing and understanding my words, in remembering them, he'd somehow integrated them into his algorithm. I wasn't such a bad pedagogue, after all! But my words had made him mischievous. They played havoc with the programmers' mathematics and physics. I confirmed my hunch when Sharon went on break and Robby performed like clockwork. As soon as she was back on the job, his wrecking spree started again. Don't ask me how the sight of a lovely girl can influence a robot. I have no idea, but I have my proof that it can. I suppose, knowing that something mysterious may happen without knowing how it happens is at the core of metaphysics. Or, in more ordinary language, it's a mystery, an enigma. It's magic.

The head programmer hinted that Robby would have to be replaced, but I'd grown fond of him. He was my student, after all, so I started thinking about how to set the programmer's brain on the right track, so that he could discover Robby's problem for himself. I would have to employ the precise science of physics; he wouldn't believe anything else. I suggested that he analyze the correlation of Robby's mishaps with the break times of workers within a hundred-foot radius. 'The results will either solve your problem,' I said, 'or send you to an asylum.' He spent a whole day pondering my suggestion, then decided to go for it. The numbers spoke for themselves: as long as Sharon was out of sight, Robby worked like a sober Fordmate; with her in view, he behaved like an inebriated, love-befuddled fumbler. The coefficient of positive correlation was as close to one as you could wish for.

Now the programmer's head was really buzzing. He went to talk to Sharon and made the mistake of asking what kind of bra and panties she wore. That earned him a slap in the face. It was only with his face smarting that he explained the possibility that static generated by synthetic material in her underwear might confuse Robby's circuits. No, she said, her preference was for cotton.

Poor programmer. He'd never had to wrestle with abstractions. He'd always trusted numbers. Numbers didn't lie. But in the end, he conceived and tested a hypothesis. He contacted the supervisor of the neighbouring line and asked him to move Sharon to a different job for two days. Robby worked through those two days without mishap; he didn't break a single windshield. To be absolutely sure his interpretation was correct, the programmer brought Sharon in and put her next to Robby. He started breaking windshields right on the stack, before he even placed them on the car. The white-shirts led her away as fast as they could, saying that she was never to come near Robby or any other robot for that matter. She agreed, readily and with a smile. She had no need to charm robots, having never lacked for human admirers.

The mystery of Robby, though solved, had remained impenetrable. There could be no doubt that Sharon's presence was the problem, and yet the solution to remove her from Robby's proximity, or else replace Robby altogether, seemed so illogical, so unfathomable, so ... metaphysical. The cost of broken windshields had climbed close to two million dollars, but Robby himself had cost almost half a million—rather expensive to be considered junk. The head programmer needed to find another, more logical, solution. Just as physicians consult about VIP patients, or try to minimize personal responsibility by hiding behind collective decisions, he called a counsel of his colleagues. He presented the numbers, explained his hypothesis, repeated the results of his experiment with Robby and Sharon before the group. They brought in coffee, sat at a picnic table loaded with paper, chewed on the numbers. They talked. Then they decided as follows: *The robot exhibits moments of inexplicable irrationality when it not only fails to follow its programming, but starts behaving contrary to its algorithm. The reasons for this anomaly can't be definitively ascertained.* They all signed the report and directed it to management, with a copy to the manufacturer.

In the end, Robby was replaced, even though he had behaved impeccably after Sharon moved to a different job. He never broke more than three windshields, and then only when a pretty girl walked by. But despite keeping a close eye on his work, the programmers had lost their trust in him. Spooked by the unfathomable unknown, they had no idea how best to handle him. For a few days, Robby was left standing a few steps away from the line, an outcast in a place of shame, while I resumed his job. My job. His posture seemed somehow stooped, resigned, his one arm touching the floor. My first and only student. From time to time I spoke a few words to him, tried to give him some comfort. Then they took him away for good.

Robby had ceased to be reliable and predictable—a fatal flaw in a robot. Nobody told me where they took him, but I think he must have ended up incarcerated in an institution for robots that cross the line between physics and metaphysics. There, he was no doubt examined by doctors in white lab coats, scientists who knocked him below the knee with a little rubber hammer and psychoanalyzed his motherboard and memory units. What conclusion those doctors might reach about Robby, I don't know. I would suggest that he was infected with the disease of common humanity.

THE HUNTING FORKLIFTS

Amid the cacophony of the plant, Joe could not possibly have heard the splat on the concrete floor, but he did notice, out of the corner of his eye, that a yellowish-brown thing had slid off the top of the cardboard box he had just pulled out of the semi-trailer. He reversed just a little more, and to the side, so he could get a better look at what it was. On the concrete floor lay a snake, probably two metres in length. Actually, it was no longer lying there—it had recovered a bit from the fall and was slowly slithering away, maybe to a safer location. The slither was somewhat jerky and it occurred to Joe that the snake was limping, supposing a snake could limp. It limped across the few metres to the wall of the third of four loading docks where it coiled itself under a sort of desk—a sheet-metal construction consisting of four short legs and a cabinet, topped by a slanted writing surface and a backboard full of pigeonholes for various forms. It was the material-handling supervisor's work-station.

Only the tip of the tail was protruding when Joe carefully approached. It was a rattler, he knew, even though, in all the noise, the rattle could only be seen, not heard. Joe drove his forklift away from the snake, then stopped to peek into the box full of wiring harnesses, still on his forks, to see if there were any more beasties inside, then laid the box aside. First the snake, then the box, he told himself. Snakes are dangerous, boxes aren't.

'Whatcha gawkin' at?' Larry had just backed out of the neighbouring loading bay with a box of different parts and now appeared beside him.

'I do believe they sent us a snake. A rattlesnake.'

Larry giggled. 'How many beers did you have for dinner?'

'One. I'm not drunk! Just take a look under Rick's desk.'

Larry dismounted and went to have a look. 'Don't get so close!' said Joe. 'Honestly, I'm not dreaming this. There's a rattlesnake under there.' Larry just waved his arm, but slowed down anyway. Still at a respectful distance, he knelt on one knee and lowered his head to get a better look. 'Something's there,' he confirmed, 'but it's so dark, I can't make it out.'

'A snake. I'm telling you. Yellowish brown. It's shaking its tail. It's gotta be a rattler. It fell from the box when I was taking it out and hit a bump. Those harnesses came from down south, you know. Some hot place like Arizona, New or old Mexico. Rattlesnakes prefer to live in warmer climates.'

'Yeah, yeah. And one wanted to emigrate, so it let itself be packed with wiring harnesses and shipped up north,' said Larry, still chuckling. 'Those harnesses do look a little like snakes. Maybe its eyesight was poor and it wanted to make friends.'

'Forgot its glasses,' Joe added.

'If it hadn't, it'd be a spectacled cobra.'

'I'm glad you've stopped thinking I'm trying to pull a prank on you.'

'All I've done so far is admit that there's something under that table. Something. I still have no idea what. Could be a pair of Rick's old socks for all I know. Just wait a minute, I'll have a better look.' From a pouch on his forklift, Larry took out the small pair of binoculars he used when he had to read small numbers, or verify a label on some crate on the upper fourth row of racks, when his regular glasses were insufficient. He knelt again and aimed them at a point underneath the supervisor's desk. 'It's not socks,' he announced, 'but it could be a harness. No, it just moved. A little, but it did move. Looks like it's alive.' Larry suddenly leapt up and yelped, 'It *is* a rattler!' From under the table the tail of the snake appeared, rattle and all. Every man there knew the sound, even though they'd never heard it except in movies. 'You were right, Joe. You were right! What're we gonna do?'

Joe scratched his head. 'We can't just leave it here. It's a dangerous creature, and it could get to the line. So far it looks like it's stupefied by the long journey, but after it warms up.... Ever hunt snakes, Larry? They're damn fast.'

'What's with the gathering?' asked a booming voice. Rick, the supervisor, arrived on his electric three-wheeler. He dismounted and started to place a bundle of papers on his desk. As one, his subordinates yelled, 'Stop!' Rick halted mid-step, one foot dangling in the air. He looked like a hunting dog. He turned his head towards them. 'What?'

'You have a rattlesnake under your desk,' said Joe.

'Get real. It's not April first. Halloween's already past. I've got no patience for pranks.'

Larry passed him the binoculars without a word. Rick looked, nodded, became more serious, scratched his chin, and resolutely stated, 'We're going to have to call the Emergency Response Team. We can't meddle with this. Into this we cannot meddle.'

'What good will they do?' Larry snickered. 'You don't think they've been trained to catch snakes here in Ontario. Not many rattlesnakes in our neck of the woods, as far as I know. Those emergency folks are only good for shutting down the plant when someone spills some chemical or gas. And they take their sweet time, too. It takes them all night to neutralize and clean up a mess.'

'We're going to have to be the ones to do something,' Joe suggested tentatively.

'Go ahead, but leave me out of it,' Larry protested. 'No one has trained me to go around chasing snakes. Not in my job description.'

'Calling the Emergency Response Team is certainly the correct procedure,' said Rick.

'Feel free to open the Standard Operating Procedures,' said Joe.

'Find section 18, paragraph 2A: "What to do when a rattlesnake endangers the workers of Ford." '

Rick wavered. 'The S.O.P.s are inside the desk, and I'm not getting near that thing, not with a rattler under it.' None of his training had ever mentioned catching snakes, either. Not even the safety briefings. The snake was a real safety hazard, though, so he decided to handle the problem in the classic way: by reporting it to a higher authority. That was surely in those S.O.P.s. In the event of a locally insoluble problem, resort to the Emergency Response Team. He reached for his walkie-talkie.

Larry held up a finger. 'I can tell you what's going to happen if you call in the team,' he said. 'They'll arrive after half an hour, discover that the issue is a snake, not chemical in nature. Then they'll spend the next half hour in consultations before calling Animal Control in Saint Thomas. No one will be there, of course, since it's the middle of the night, so the Emergency Response Team will close the plant and send everyone home, including the morning shift. In the morning, Animal Control will begin to hunt for the snake, but by that time, they'll have to search the entire plant, because that snake will be warmed up by then, and it certainly won't be waiting around for them under this table. And, of course, there's the possibility that Animal Control will discover it's some endangered species of rattler, declare this plant its natural habitat, and close the plant down for good. No, Rick. I hate to say it, but we're going to have to save this plant ourselves.'

'What's going on here, guys?' This was Hubert, another lift-truck operator, just arrived from the cafeteria. 'You can take your break now, Joe,' he said.

'Out of the question!' Joe proclaimed. 'We have a problem. They sent us a rattlesnake from down South. There it is, hiding under Rick's desk. We'll have to hunt it. You're a hunter, do you have any tips on how to go about it?'

'What do you need tips for?' asked Hubert, 'I'll just go out to my truck, grab my shotgun and pump it full of birdshot. I'll be right back.'

'Stop, you idiot!' Rick thundered. 'You can't bring a firearm into the plant, much less start shooting!'

'Come on, this is an exceptional circumstance!' said Hubert. 'Public safety.'

'And there'll be an investigation, and they'll find you had a loaded gun in your truck instead of somewhere in your basement under lock and key. They'll find you had the ammo with it, instead of under a different lock and key somewhere in your attic, like the law requires. The bureaucrats would devour you alive for discharging a weapon in the plant. Jesus, they'd make an example of you. Do you want to get your gun confiscated and yourself fined or jailed? You want that? Just sit here and help us think of a way to get the snake without shooting it.' To calm himself, Rick lit a cigarette.

Hubert sat down in eloquent silence.

'We can't just let some snake stop the whole plant,' said Joe.

'Look, those harnesses are your business, Joe,' said Rick. 'Go and finish unloading them.'

'You know what? No,' said Joe categorically. 'I read in *Huckleberry Finn* that rattlesnakes typically appear in pairs. If I go to unload them, there'll be another one. It'll jump out at me from the top row. Do you suppose the medic here has anti-venom? Realistically, before we start this hunt, shouldn't we contact Medical in case something goes wrong? Have an ambulance and such ready?'

'All they'd do is get in our way, telling us "no this" and "no that", and "be careful" ...'

Rick massaged his forehead. 'Who else could possibly help us?'

'I understand we have an archery champion here,' Larry offered. 'An older fellow. He works somewhere in shipping.'

Hubert piped up, irate. 'And I'm sure he brings his bow and arrows to work in his lunch box. Why would he be allowed to shoot stuff in here, but not me with my Remington?'

'Maybe he has the bow in his car,' Rick countered. 'If I remember right, the S.O.P. is explicit about firearms, but it says nothing specific about bows and arrows, so we might be able to get away with it.'

'You shoot a bow same as a gun,' declared Hubert. 'You might as well ask whatshisname, the black belt martial artist. I don't know which line he works on. Maybe he'd like to engage in close combat with the rattler. Maybe he could kick its ass.'

'If he could find the snake's ass, maybe,' Joe remarked.

Rick brought the conversation back to earth. 'Stop fooling around, gents, we're trying to solve a serious problem here.'

'What do you think?' asked Larry. 'Can a rattlesnake leap into the air? Or spit poison at a distance? Some snakes can.'

'Who knows.'

'Surely,' Rick said with a sigh, 'surely there's someone on the line who's run into rattlesnakes in his life. Plenty of people in the plant from tropical areas who'd know. But how would we find them in a hurry?'

'Human Resources could tell us. Same with the archery champ and the black belt,' Larry suggested.

'This discussion is getting us nowhere. I'm going for my gun,' Hubert declared. 'It's the best way to hunt. Don't let the target get close. Then bang! The end, no matter how much that snake tries to slither around.'

'Shut up!' said Rick. 'You are not getting the gun. We've got to figure out some way to render it harmless.'

'Christ almighty,' said Joe. 'This is a first for the plant. There've been plenty of calamities, but no snakes until today.'

Larry scratched his head. 'How could it have gotten into the box? It was definitely not packed intentionally. Do snakes normally just slither into factories and start making friends with wiring harnesses?'

'Certainly not. No one could work like that,' said Rick,

thinking it over. 'Maybe they took one of the finished boxes out to the yard to wait for shipping. If the sun's hot enough, maybe a snake would crawl into a box, not expecting to be driven north for two days and two nights while the weather gets colder and colder until it's positively frigid....'

'Do you remember the time we were snowed-in here and no one could go home for thirty hours,' said Joe.

'Of course. We all remember that,' said Larry dreamily. 'That was a real crisis.'

'When was that, anyway?' Joe said. 'In seventy-seven or eight, I think. A metre of snow overnight. We ate the cafeteria out of food. People were sleeping in the back seats of finished cars. Some ran out of cigarettes and got nasty. Andy sat playing poker in the cafeteria the whole time and lost nearly ten grand.'

Rick stomped his foot. 'Enough! Look, guys, we've been rambling on about nothing, and we're missing the damned point. That snake is going to warm up, and when it does, it will become faster and more dangerous. We have to catch it now.'

'That's what I said,' said Joe. 'You heard me, Larry. I said that snake is going to warm up. I said ...'

'Will you shut your effin' mouth, Joseph!' said Rick.

'How about to start the hunt by turning off the curtain of warm air between the relative heat of the factory and the relative cool of the semi-trailer,' said Joe.

'Shouldn't we at least call the general foreman,' asked Hubert hopefully, 'so he at least knows about this? Maybe he'd let me use my gun.' Rick raised his hands and his eyes to the ceiling.

'He'll permit you squat,' Larry proclaimed. 'He won't take responsibility for this fiasco. He'll call the general engineer, who'll call the plant manager—it's two in the morning, remember—and *he'll* have to decide, unless he decides to call Mr Ford himself in Detroit. But you can't call anyone, anyways, because your telephone is on your desk and there's a rattler under your desk. No, better to handle this ourselves. What if the general foreman shuts down our whole hunt?'

Rick cradled his head in his hands. 'That might just be for the better.'

'We discovered the snake,' said Joe. 'This is our snake. It's our hunt. We're not letting anyone else get in our way.'

'Leave me out of it,' said Larry in a low voice. 'I can't handle the sight of blood.'

'Are you suggesting that we catch it alive?'

'Even a drop of blood makes me faint. I'll fall off my truck, straight into the snake's path, and it'll bite me.'

'If you faint, you'll be stiff as a board. The snake will slither right over you without biting,' said Hubert teasingly. He and Larry were old friends. They ribbed each other all the time. 'What kind of crap is this, anyway? Since when are you so blood-shy? How many times have I seen you smash a mosquito into a bloody mess without fainting? Why don't you just admit you haven't got the guts to hunt anything bigger?'

'I've got more courage than you can even dream of,' retorted Larry. 'You with your long-distance rifle hunting. Put a lion under that desk and I'd lead the charge, even though I've never hunted anything bigger than a mouse. With a trap. I just can't stand snakes. They have such a cold stare,' he added with a shudder.

'Oh, I see. You're Indiana Jones.'

'Thanks for that. Why not, Indiana Jones was no coward. Still, just leave me out of this hunt.'

'Impossible,' said Rick, pensively. 'This is an emergency. We're going to need all hands on deck.'

Larry just shook his head and addressed himself to Joe, nervous now. 'You've never hunted either, have you? But look at you now—so eager that your eyes are practically shining with glee. I don't recognize you. Where's the thoughtful, deliberate Joe I used to know? Where has that one gone?'

'True, I've never hunted, but maybe that's the point. I want the excitement at least once. I need it!' Joe looked almost wild with excitement. 'Look, ever since I climbed into my forklift for the first time some fifteen years ago, all I've done, all I ever do, day after day, is feed the line, unload the railway cars, unload the semis, load empty baskets, bring stuff here, carry stuff there, place, replace, displace, lift to a rack, lower from a rack, deliver this to column D14. Day after day, week after week, year after year. Boring! Fifteen years of soul-crushing boredom. Until today. Today we've been delivered a gift—a break from routine. You bet I'm gung-ho! Enjoy the occasion, man. Have you never felt like a knight on a warhorse, driving your machine? I used to, many times, back when I was younger. And now I find myself with a chance to ride my trusty steed in pursuit of a dragon. I'm going to skewer the beast with my fork, just like Saint George.'

'You've got a point, Joe. Sort of. But a snake ... I don't like it.'

'We need your help, Larry,' said Joe, looking at Rick. 'The snake might escape if we don't surround him. Please.'

'OK, you asked for it,' said Rick resolutely, pointing at Larry. 'As your supervisor, I order you to co-operate in removing the hazard represented by this poisonous snake. When we go into action, I order you to fasten your seat belt to keep from fainting, falling off your machine, and hitting the concrete floor. Here we go.'

'An order is an order, boss,' Larry mumbled.

'We shouldn't give it a chance to warm up too much. Let's get at it.'

'We've been going at it for twenty minutes already, and we're still standing here,' remarked Joe. 'But I have a plan. Since Larry here is the careful one, he'll fork the table up from the front. Once the snake is exposed I'll drop my fork on it. So it can't escape, Hubert will block its way with his machine.'

'I still think we should shoot it', muttered Hubert. 'A hunt without shooting is not a hunt. Poaching, maybe, but not hunting.

'You'll stay here,' Rick ordered. 'It's your responsibility to keep it from escaping to the right. Joe will cut off its escape to the left and smash it. Or if it comes your way, you smash it. I'll be coordinating the whole operation from over here. It's as good as dead. Ready? Let's go. Larry, time to lift.'

Four pairs of eyes lit up. Larry buckled his seatbelt. Joe's fingers were dancing along his steering wheel. Hubert was still muttering about his gun, but he was also ready. Their breathing sped up with the atavistic excitement of the hunt. Adrenaline focused their attention, sharpened their thoughts.

'Are you guys sure it can't jump?' asked Larry, one last time.

'It can't. Snakes don't have legs. And it'll be sluggish in this cold. It's about ten degrees outside, and here in the docking bay it's not much more than fifteen. That snake is shivering in the cold and thinking it should have stayed home.'

Larry slowly and carefully manoeuvred his forklift up to the desk and slid the forks under it. They were all scarcely breathing now. Rick stood in his three-wheeler, shielding his eyes. Joe and Hubert raised their forks a few centimetres above the floor, ready to bring them down on the intruder. Larry raised the table slowly, so as to not frighten or aggravate the snake. When he had raised the table half a metre, Joe yelled, 'It's not there!'

'He escaped!' shouted Hubert.

'What?' exclaimed Rick in disbelief. 'What do you mean "escaped"? It can't have escaped. We've been here the whole time.'

Hubert couldn't resist needling him. 'Was anyone keeping an eye on it?'

'Now the real chase begins,' said Joe. 'It must have headed for the line. It's warmer there under all the lights. After him!'

'I'll head up to the line foreman and let him know to warn his people,' said Rick. 'Good God, this is an effing disaster.'

Three forklifts set out in the access aisle next to the line. Three sets of peeled eyes examined every crack and crevice between boxes, every dark corner under the shelves along the walls. After some forty metres, they arrived at Reggie, the forklift guy responsible for feeding materials to the line.

'You'll never believe what just happened!' he shouted, standing beside his machine. 'I'm backing up from the line and what do I see in front of me? A snake! A real snake! A little flat, granted, since I ran over it backing up, but still recognizable. So I ran over it again, just to be sure. A snake doesn't belong in the plant. Just imagine what kind of havoc it could cause.' He paused. 'Hey, what's with you guys? You look like I rained on your parade.'

'That was our snake,' Joe said stonily. 'We were on its trail. It wouldn't have escaped us.' He sighed. 'Well, it had to be kept away from the line. So good for you, I guess.'

The adrenaline drained away. Larry, Joe, and Hubert turned their machines around. Slowly and silently, they returned to the docking bay. Finally, Hubert said, 'You can go on your break now, Joe. Now you can.'

Joe just shook his head. 'That fool ruined our fun.' But after a long pause, and with a slight lift in his voice, he added, 'You know, they say rattlesnakes travel in pairs. We're going to be unloading the rest of those harnesses. Maybe we'll be lucky and find another.'

HAVE YOU DRIVEN A FORD ... LATELY

'Have you driven a Ford ... lately?' So warbled the angelic female voices in the latest Ford commercial. Chuck turned off the TV, grumbling. 'You bet your sorry ass I have. In a minute, I'll be driving a Ford to the Ford plant where the Ford Motor Company's production line will continue to drive me out of my mind.' Chuck had been in a morose mood for the last three weeks, and the very idea of another shift on the line made him feel like a pressure cooker with a stuck valve. He grabbed his lunch box and backpack, locked the door of his apartment, rode the elevator down to the parking lot, and got behind the wheel. On his way to work he stopped at The Beer Store. He would certainly need a drink today, with the humidex hovering around forty. He'd be dripping sweat like water from a showerhead. Well, he'd have to survive somehow. The two-four would help.

The concrete in the parking lot at the plant was ablaze. Fordmates joked that it's the hottest place on the earth, outscorching Death Valley by a hell and a half. Chuck was reluctant to leave his air-conditioned vehicle. For a moment, he considered going back home, even if it cost him an unauthorized absence, but he opened the door and stepped out. He wasn't one for absences, let alone unauthorized ones. Leaning over the backseat, he transferred the beer from the carton to his backpack before walking into the plant. In the locker room, he decided today was definitely no day for coveralls. He would work in shorts and a T-shirt, so he merely switched his sneakers for safety shoes.

His workstation was in a distant corner of the plant. It took him nearly five minutes to reach it. Under the roof, the haze-like heat was even worse than it was outside. He nodded to his opposite from the other shift, grabbed his cooler from under the table and went for ice. Luckily, last summer the Company had installed 'hydration stations' with cold water and ice machines. He buried a few cans of beer under the ice in the cooler and kept one out to drink it right away. He slid the can into a foam sleeve that read Pepsi to hide it from the supervisor. He still had five free minutes, plenty to finish the beer. He had a deal with his opposite: the guy coming in for the night shift lets the other guy go fifteen minutes before the buzzer. Chuck was there, anyway, and it was sensible to let the tired guy go a few minutes early.

'How was it today?' he asked, preparing to take over.

'Brutal. Can't wait for a shower and a pitcher of cold beer.'

'Have a cold one for me as well,' said Chuck. 'See ya tomorrow.'

Chuck settled in, then reached into his cooler for another beer. Again, the beer can had to pretend it was Pepsi. He had several such sleeves to camouflage his beer, all of them advertising non-alcoholic beverages. Drinking on the line was prohibited, but when the beer can was discreetly hidden, nobody cared too much. The beer hadn't properly cooled yet, but Chuck couldn't wait.

Three turns of a long bolt into the thread of the F-mount. Tighten the three bolts of the motor mount with the gun, then pick up the so-called A-frame, the upper arm to secure the front wheel. Carry it on a special holder along to the car frame, position it correctly, push two bolts through the provided holes, and hand start the nuts. Done. Repeat. Two workstations down the line, Adrian will tighten those two nuts, then add the lower arm, then connect both arms. After that, it's brake rotors and calipers, and finally, somewhere towards the end of line three, the whole front wheel will be installed. Chuck was pleased to be working at the very beginning of the whole process. He felt like he was laying the cornerstone for some magnificent edifice. His A-frames were sub-assembled off the line and reached him on an inclined mini line, moving along by their own weight. There were two catches to this job: the big car frames, moving sideways on two oversized bicycle chains, were a bit too high for Chuck, their height off the floor having been dictated by averaging the requirements of all jobs on both sides of the line. Chuck would have welcomed the frames coming at him about four inches lower. Being of average height, he had to lift the A-frames to hook them to the car frame, and had to do the lifting more or less one-armed. Not an easy task, considering that each A-frame weighed thirty-two pounds. His left shoulder and his back were constantly sore—and no wonder, after more than two years on this killer job.

Chuck had survived a couple of other killer jobs before. For a while he'd managed to snag a relatively decent job installing shock absorbers, but not for long. Three years ago, robots invaded the body shop and four hundred people were laid off. Chuck had been among them. He'd spent more than half a year at home, quite content. He rested, healed, rebuilt his energy. He was recalled two years ago, in early May. Normally, each May, the company hired students to cover for people going on vacation, but that year no students were hired. Laid off workers had to be recalled first. Chuck landed his current killer job because, after the layoff, he had slipped to the bottom rung of the seniority ladder. After two very long years, he'd been hoping that this summer he might be released. The students were back, and the supervisor had promised him that he'd let a student hoist the A-frames, so Chuck could get some relief on a relatively easier job somewhere else on the line. At least for those four summer months. Chuck had been counting on the coming relief for the last two months. He'd been surviving on that hope.

The students came, and two were assigned to Chuck's zone of the line. Two girls. Chuck frowned. He reached into his cooler and polished off a beer in one gulp. With a curt nod, he acknowledged the greeting of the girl now working across the line from him. She was installing two arms to carry the rear axle, a dream job that required a mere seven or ten pounds of lifting per arm. Chuck might have had that job if the supervisor hadn't betrayed him. But there would be no relief forthcoming for him. Pain or no pain, he'd have to soldier on with A-frames for at least a third summer.

It wasn't betrayal, not exactly. The supervisor had no choice. Labour Relations had sent him two girls, and two girls, each weighing maybe fifty kilos soaking wet, after a big dinner, couldn't be expected to lift and carry a thirty-two-pound A-frame once every sixty seconds. But Chuck felt he'd earned a break from his killer job, and resented his supervisor for not fighting hard enough to get him some relief. The fellow ought to have barged into Labour Relations and pounded on a desk until they agreed to give him someone capable of doing the heavy lifting. Of course, Chuck didn't know that a supervisor who wants to remain a supervisor is in no position to bang any desk that's not his own.

Chuck knew it was theoretically possible to escape a killer job. He recalled with a smile the experience of his friend Howard, who'd spent years on the pedestal line. But Howard had gotten out—he'd found a way to penetrate the indifference—or was it ignorance—of the higher-ups. A while back, Howard had been installing steering boxes. This involved grabbing the sub-assembled box, carrying it to the frame, setting it on a steering linkage, and hand starting the securing bolts. He'd been on that job for well over two years and his body was so worn out that it occasionally failed to execute the orders of his brain. Twice, towards the end of a shift, the steering box had slipped from his hands, and he'd barely managed to jump aside and avoid crushing his feet. He went to Medical. The doctor listened to him, felt his muscles, but failed to find any specific injury. Lifting heavy objects was part of working at Ford, wasn't it? So was tiredness. He hinted at the need for Howard to mobilize his inner toughness and try again. Howard tried. The very next day, a steering box once again slipped out of his hands. He went to Medical again, but this time he didn't go empty handed. With a length of rope, he dragged a steering box behind him. He looked like a god of revenge walking a dachshund. People laughed as he passed. When he got to Medical he didn't have to wait. As soon as the nurse noticed his companion, she ushered him into the doctor's office and remained standing in the doorway, partly out of curiosity, partly in case she needed to call for help.

'What's that supposed to be?' the doctor asked, curious, while trying to recall his basic psychiatric training. 'Does it bite?'

'It's a steering box, doc,' scoffed Howard. 'I'd like you to lift it waist high, carry it over there, hold it for a second in one hand, then place it, gently, on that examination table.'

The doctor bent over and grabbed the monster. He was pushing fifty and didn't look particularly strong. The nurse watched with amusement.

'Careful,' Howard advised. 'It's much heavier than it looks.'

The doctor adjusted his stance, lifted, and with some huffing carried the box to the table. 'You forgot the one-handed part,' Howard said. 'I guess you didn't want to drop it and break all those nice tiles on the floor.' The doctor was massaging his forearm.

'Yesterday, forty-five pounds was just a number to you. Now you *know*, doctor, what it really feels like.' Howard was giving the doctor a hard stare. 'But you only had to lift it once. I lift it five hundred times a day, which adds up to some twenty-two thousand pounds per shift. I've been doing this for more than two years. My will is strong enough, doc, but my hands refuse to obey. The inner toughness you prescribed seems to have been exhausted.'

The doctor blinked, sat down at his computer, and handed Howard a signed, month-long exemption from his job.

So Howard had escaped his killer job, but Chuck was doubtful the trick would work for a second time with the same doctor. His A-frames were fourteen pounds lighter than Howard's steering boxes, and he was missing a certain key ingredient: he wasn't mad enough yet. Not quite. 'I was ready to throw that thing at his head,' Howard had confided at the time of his liberation, 'and the doctor could read it in my eyes.' Chuck was not yet that far gone. When his body completely lacked the strength to carry out the orders of his brain, he might reconsider—though he would really like to remind the higher-ups that vague terms like 'A-frame' and 'steering box', so abstract on a computer screen, have very specific, weighty, and often painful meanings for the real workers on the line.

With his hopes for an exit from A-frames collapsed, Chuck felt like an inmate in a jail. He was permanently and majorly tense. Angry! That called for another beer, quick, because Chuck knew where his thoughts were heading. The whole situation was unfair, and the unfairness was turning him into a walking, smoking volcano. He was worried about a heart attack—high blood pressure in this heat could be lethal. He wouldn't be the first to be hauled off the line in an ambulance. Aside from his health concerns, he was afraid that he might one day snap and attack somebody, bite them or beat them with an A-frame. What if his rage built up until it blasted him into a thousand pieces? The girl whose job he coveted was within view for the entirety of his shift, and seeing her stoked the flames of his anger. Luckily, he had discovered that beer acted as a sort of medicine, a sedative to blunt the edge of his resentment. He visited The Beer Store every day now.

Under the influence, his thinking took some interesting shortcuts, ones that would be unthinkable without the wonderful hoppy brew. For example, he noticed that the woman who had landed the plum axle arms job would, like him, hit the bottom of the barrel from time to time. She might be a victim of the same system. She had been ordered here, and her orders meant that he was not released from his A-frame job as he should have been.

She was a victim of the same system built on a claim that men and women had the same abilities across the board. Slogans! Damned slogans! 'Men and women are the same.' 'Women can do anything men do.' 'A woman can do just as well, or better, whatever a man does.' Such proclamations were in newspapers, radio, TV. They rubbed Chuck the wrong way as they ran contrary to his experience. Yet, despite their obvious fallacy, the government decided to act upon them and force employers to change their hiring policies. All in the name of fairness. To deal with the fallout, and to reconcile the wishful thinking of the slogan makers with real life, fell on the Company, the hired women as well as people like Chuck and his buddies on the line.

Unlike the slogan creators, those in the plant knew that you couldn't put a woman on engine decking, A-frames, or steering boxes—you had to find easier jobs for them. It resulted in screwing up the whole time-honoured seniority system in which new hires got the toughest jobs and those with more years on the line climbed the ladder to the easier ones. Without the young backs arriving to take their place, the guys on killer jobs had to stay much longer than was bearable. The number of injuries went up. How can this be fair? Chuck thought. We are the same, we are able to do the same thing. Bullshit! And if we are the same, why has the atmosphere in the plant changed so much? Chuck couldn't let off steam by using four letter words, or telling sex jokes, or reading Playboy on his breaks, or scratching himself in certain places. He always felt he had to be careful who he looked at and how. 'We are the same. Are we? Bullshit and more bullshit.

But the unfairness didn't end there. The summer students completely dismantled the standard of equal pay for equal work. Students worked only four months a year and didn't make enough to pay any tax, so they took home about thirty percent more per hour than Chuck. Everything was a fraud and a lie.

The whole system sat oppressively on his shoulders. It was the fault of the higher-ups. The powers that be. The category encompassed just about everyone above his supervisor—the general foreman, the chief engineer, the plant manager, all the way up to, heck, even up to the government. Chuck felt helpless against them all. He was turning into a permanently angry young man, at loggerheads with any authority, because he considered most authority to be inherently unfair. His ordeal was pushing him dangerously close to anarchism. Even his favourite heroes, like commando-playing Arnold Schwarzenegger, or kick-ass Jean-Claude Van Damme, would fail against this system. Whose face would Arnold smash when the system was faceless? Whose ass would Van Damme kick when the system, though full of assholes, had no ass? For Chuck, the system was a chimera made of paper: regulations, directions, procedures, proclamations, laws. Anonymous, lifeless paper. It didn't care about fairness or justice.

From experience, Chuck knew that this kind of thinking heralded the riskiest stretch of his workday. If he were to suffer a heart attack, it would be about now. If he were to grab an A-frame and throw it at somebody, or run around waving it above his head like a club, now would be the time. If his mind was going to explode, or implode in a stroke, it would be right about now. To prevent further escalation of his fury and defuse any potential aggression, he had to guzzle another beer. The longer he worked, the more he guzzled.

More than a few times, the thought crossed his mind that he might be better off on welfare. He knew of people, people with high seniority even, who had reached the breaking point on the line. They quit their jobs and, after their unemployment ran out, settled down on welfare. They lived on less money than they had at Ford, but they had more time, more energy, more freedom. Had Chuck gone the same route, he would this very moment have been on a beach among the girls in bikinis, not coveralls. He'd be cooling himself by swimming in Lake Erie, not by dipping into a cooler for another beer. His shoulders wouldn't be hurting. He wouldn't be so frickin' pissed off all the time. But so far, he'd resisted the temptation. He couldn't stand the thought of living at someone else's expense. Living on welfare would mean resigning his independence, giving up control of his own life. Sooner or later, he wanted to marry, to have a family, to be able to provide for that family. So he clenched his teeth, lifted one A-frame after another, cursed, sweated, and guzzled.

Finally, the beer started to take effect. Chuck's mind floated in suds like an embryo in amniotic fluid. From now until the end of the shift, everything should sail along smoothly, as long as he didn't allow his alcohol level to drop low enough to permit his mind to run aground on the dangerous reef of thought. The world started to smile at him, and he smiled back. He even smiled at the student on the other side of the line. Now he remembered—her name was Joanne. He realized that she was struggling to manage the job he considered easy. Ten pounds for those slim arms must feel as heavy as thirty-two for him. He saw that her face was now and then darkened by a fleeting grimace. She was clearly in pain. She'd be better off tanning on a beach somewhere, gossiping with friends, flirting with boys. He imagined her dragging herself home after the shift, stooped and defeated. She would likely fall into bed and lose consciousness right after the shift. Her life was in hock until September. She wouldn't be able to dream about boys this summer, much less muster enough energy to smile at one. Was she just as miserable as him? Might a can of beer do her good? No, his sudden sympathy wouldn't go that far.

The buzzer! Half an hour for lunch. He'd made it this far: five hours behind him, five more ahead. About nine thousand pounds of A-frames already lifted, another nine thousand to go. Solid training for a professional weightlifter, much more than any Nautilus fitness bum could manage. Chuck bypassed the washroom; what he drank these days, he sweated out. If he didn't drink so much, he'd become dehydrated. He'd turn into a desiccated mummy before lunch. Some of his colleagues lunched in the cafeteria, some others brought a cup of coffee and congregated at a picnic table to play cards, a few could be seen sitting here and there reading a newspaper, some even tried to take a short nap lying down on the steel racks. Chuck preferred sitting on a piece of cardboard on the floor and resting his back against a big box. He ate a ham sandwich with two beers and then headed outside, a few steps from the line. It might be a bit cooler out there now, just before midnight. Yes, it was pleasant. He sat down on a patch of concrete, lit a cigarette, and looked up at the stars. They appeared a bit hazy because of the humidity. He noticed a brand-new Marquis parked not too far away. It was probably waiting for some missing part. Chuck went to investigate. Maybe he could start the car and run the air conditioning to cool off a bit. He opened the door. The inside lights went on. Good, the car had a working battery. The keys were in the ignition too, but when Chuck looked at his watch he realized he didn't have time to enjoy the cool breeze. He hurried back to the line.

The second half of Chuck's shift went swimmingly, thanks to the divine nectar that slowed his thinking and even subdued the pain in his shoulder and back. Just as a car engine needed a certain level of oil, Chuck's engine required lubrication in the form of beer. As four o'clock and the end of his shift approached, an idea hatched in his head and began to circle in his mind like a moth around a flame. Round and round it went, tirelessly, unstoppably. Why, after spending ten hours on his feet, should he be obliged to march all the way to the gates and beyond to the parking lot? Why, when a nice ride, with keys already in the ignition, was right outside the door, just waiting for him? That ride could save him a thousand steps and at least five minutes. He'd park the vehicle right inside the gate. Either someone would find it there in the morning, and bring it back here, or he'd use it again to return before the next shift. The longer the idea circulated in his head, the more he liked it. His feet hurt, his back was in flames, the car was sitting there. All he needed to do was turn the key.

After the buzzer, he grabbed his backpack, now full of empty cans, and his lunch box. He'd empty the cooler tomorrow, when he refilled it with fresh ice. Instead of heading over the line and into the locker room, he went the other way—to the Marquis. It was still there. He threw his backpack into the backseat, slipped behind the wheel, turned the key in the ignition. The engine came alive. Hurrah! He shifted into drive, released the parking brake, and off she went. He didn't go too fast—no more than fifty, maybe sixty. He had a fuzzy sense of having killed a lot of beers. In a minute, he was in the front yard. Crowds of people were emerging from the locker room and hurrying across the yard to the gate, to make it home as quickly as possible. He hit the brakes. Nothing! Again! Nothing! Damn it, there were no brakes. He was going to hurt or even kill somebody. At the last moment, he swerved the car and crashed it under a trailer parked at the loading dock. Boom! The airbag erupted, pinning him to the seat. By some miracle, he was unhurt. In an instant, he was sober. He knew he had to climb out of the wreck and disappear into the crowd. But before he could extricate himself, two security guards grabbed him and pulled him out. Two more guards ran up from the security house by the gate. Chuck didn't have the energy to fight them off or run away.

Resigned to his fate, he let them to deliver him to Medical. The nurses were grumpy; their shift was over too. But they checked him out, tended to a few bruises, and took his blood for the alcohol test. Then they confiscated his own car keys and called a taxi to haul him off to bed.

Long after noon the following day, Chuck emerged from his unconscious state, not quite sure how he'd gotten home. He knew he was in deep shit, but somehow he couldn't recall the details. Should he go to work? He decided against it. He couldn't risk it until he remembered what he had done—or until somebody told him. At about seven o'clock in the evening, he got a call from Labour Relations. Where was he? Why hadn't he reported for work? They told him to stay home for the night, but tomorrow, right at the beginning of the shift, he was to report to Labour Relations and explain his behaviour. A case against him had been opened. There would be an investigation. He could lose his job. The call completely swept away all the residual mist in Chuck's head. He was beyond sober. He was in danger of ending up on the extended holiday of welfare, regardless of his determination to avoid it. If anything could save him, it was his Union. He made a phone call to his Union rep to arrange a meeting for the next day, a consultation to take place right before the interrogation at Labour Relations.

At the meeting, he explained in great detail his reasons for excessive consumption of beer on the assembly line—it was vital to prevent possible aggression on his part, not to mention necessary to ward off the dangers of dehydration. He discussed the unfairness of the system, his supervisor, the Company, and society as a whole.

The Union rep just kept shaking his head. He promised Chuck that the Union would fight for him, though it would be a tough battle. 'It doesn't look good, brother,' he said. 'That car is a write-off. You dimwit, didn't you see the big orange sticker on the windshield, right above the wheel: Don't drive! Danger! No brakes! You must have been completely wasted.' But beyond his dimwittedness, the Union rep made sure to make Chuck aware of his social faux pas. 'By the way, do you know what all the guys who work next to you are saying, brother? That you're a pig! Yes, brother, a selfish pig. You brought in twenty-four cans of beer and didn't share a one. Not a single one. Pig. Gluttonous, boozing pig! That's what they're saying about you, brother.' He shook his head again in disapproval. 'Well, we'll see what we can do for you anyway.'

It turned out that the Union could do quite a lot. Chuck had an unblemished record, with no unauthorized absences. He'd been doing his jobs well, never letting an unfinished car pass him. He wasn't a troublemaker. Crashing that car was his first misdemeanor in six years. The good record softened the higher-ups. After pressure from the Union, the company agreed to give Chuck a second chance, but only after a four-month unpaid suspension.

Chuck would survive that. He didn't qualify for unemployment, but he had some savings to tide him over. In the end, the punishment turned out to be a very pleasant holiday. He rested at home, healing his aches and replenishing his energy levels. He spent hot days on the beach, with students who preferred enjoying their free time to making money on summer jobs, with moms and their toddlers, even with a few of those who had chosen welfare as their way of life. He drank beer only when he was really thirsty. No more than two or three cans a day.

When he reported back for work at the end of October, the supervisor called him into his little portable office. 'You lucky bastard,' he said. 'You don't really deserve this, but I've got a couple of new hires. One of them is already struggling with your upper A-frames. You'll be doing rear axles, with Amos. It's a two-man job. Hopefully, you'll be able to handle this job without booze. Amos will keep an eye on you. You've got three days for training. I'll be keeping a close watch on you. One beer on the line, one single beer, and you're out the door for good. Understood?'

'Understood, boss! And thanks!'

It was as if the wings of angels carried Chuck out of the supervisor's office. A new job! Finally, his dream had become reality. Rear axles wasn't a bad job. Pick up the axle on a hoist, deliver it to the frame, install it with the help of your partner. Easy money.

A mighty roar welcomed him back to the line. His buddies must have forgotten that he hadn't shared his beer. Or maybe they'd forgiven him. Above his new workstation they had stretched a great big white-and-blue sign: Have you driven a Ford … lately?

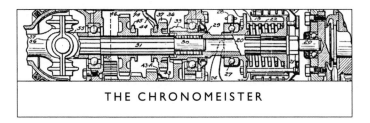

THE CHRONOMEISTER

'Yes, sir! Yes fucking way!'

The Union rep jerked his head and rolled his eyes. Had three other people not been standing in the supervisor's office, he probably would have slapped his forehead and howled in disgust at the naiveté of his charge. *What a dimwit,* he thought. *What a colossal moron, to so innocently agree with the Chronomeister's plan.* Didn't he know that *any* Company request invariably ought to be met with *No fucking way!*

The supervisor, permanent occupant of the small office, tried to keep a neutral face. *God help us,* he thought. But he had to maintain some level of decorum, so he just nodded.

The Company Time Studies engineer, generally known as the Chronomeister, smiled, anticipating no real resistance from this naive worker.

Erik, who had spoken the upsetting words, and who had the most at stake, was not completely calm, but neither was he shaking in his boots at the prospect of facing the Chronomeister. The way he intended to play the game was more important to him than how he started it. Had he opened with *No way!* as expected, he would have immediately handed the advantage over to the Chronomeister. The contract between the Company and the Union stipulated that for three months in each calendar year, management had the right to change, alter, remix, and move jobs on the line, and that every operator was required to cooperate. Had Erik refused to cooperate, the Chronomeister would have cited the contract, the Union rep would have had to concur, and Erik would have been on the defensive even before the opening moves were made. Besides, his agreement indicated only his willingness to co-operate in a time study, not his acceptance of any alterations to his job that the Chronomeister might propose. Erik was actually quite excited by the prospect of this duel, and the relief it might offer from the boredom of everyday work.

'I'll be with you in forty minutes,' the Chronomeister announced. 'You'll be back from your break, so we'll have two hours to complete the first study.' He turned on his heel and walked away, whistling softly. Little did he know ...

Erik deflected the reproaches and well-meant advice from the Union rep. It was Erik who would battle the Chronomeister; it was up to him to choose his weapons and tactics.

What was the impetus for the coming battle? The Chronomeister's habitat for nine months of the year was the engineering office, located far away from the line. The office housed a really smart computer whose memory stored descriptions of each and every job on each and every line. Each job was broken down into the movements required to complete each individual operation. Attached to every movement, every step, was a time interval measuring how long it took to perform. The sum of the time intervals was the total time a worker had to complete their assigned operation. At the present speed of the line, each job took up to fifty-six seconds. The Chronomeister played with those seconds and split seconds in an effort to reorganize and remix jobs with the goal of eliminating one or two operators per line and loading their work onto the workers who remained. Of course, the basic sequence and structure of jobs on the line was dictated by the technology of assembling a car—the installation of brakes had to precede that of wheels—but the theory was that plenty of minor stuff could be shuffled around in the interests of efficiency. Some fastener might not be needed until line five, but could perhaps be installed on line two. An operation might be streamlined or divided into sub-operations. The Chronomeister juggled and shuffled these sub-operations, saving a second here, another there, and before you knew it, he had ferreted out the fifty-six seconds required to eliminate one worker per shift. For nine months, his game of seconds occurred in virtual reality; now he had three months to prove that his calculations would work, not only on a computer screen, but also in the real world on the line.

Erik was familiar with the Chronomeister's game. When he returned to his job, he tried honestly, and just for himself, to figure out whether the Chronomeister's timesaving idea was doable. It was not. The Chronomeister would have to discover a time savings of at least four seconds in the current workflow. The Chronomeister had made a mistake, and Erik would have to discover where.

What nobody at Ford knew, or even suspected, was that Erik had a master's degree in mechanical engineering. In his homeland, he might have risen to the status of chief engineer, even manager of a Ford plant like this one, but he hadn't earned his Master's degree in Canada or the US, so nobody took it seriously. During his initial job hunt as a new immigrant, he discovered that his foreign degree made him simultaneously unqualified for some jobs and, paradoxically, overqualified for others. After a few months of beating his head on a brick wall, he accepted the real-world verdict: in the eyes of Canadian employers, he had no higher education. Must have slipped out of his pocket on his way across the Atlantic, or else customs officers confiscated it upon his arrival. So, a high school diploma was all that figured in his Ford dossier. Erik had no idea why, out of the four guys he had to choose from, the Chronomeister had picked him for the testing—his work on the passenger side of the car was the same as what his buddy did down the line on the driver's side, and two more guys performed the same tasks on the other shift. Erik actually suspected that he'd been chosen on the basis of his foreign-sounding name and accented English. For many

Canadians, accented speech subconsciously suggested less than average intelligence. The Chronomeister—an experienced, careful and thorough time-and-motion-study man—had been harassing people on the line with his stopwatch for some twenty-five years. He must have assumed Erik's accent made him less assertive than his Canadian-born counterparts, perhaps mentally on the defensive in an effort to fit in in his new homeland.

After ten years with Ford, Erik had landed a job on lower A-frames, installing the lower arm that supports the front wheel. Well, from his standpoint, it was more of an upper arm, as the whole frame arrived at his workstation upside down. Under normal circumstances, the job could be completed in an average of fifty-four seconds, while the line speed afforded fifty-six. Those two seconds had probably attracted the Chronomeister and convinced him that he could even squeeze an additional six or seven seconds out of Erik's job.

Secure in the knowledge that it could not be achieved, Erik had the next half hour to prepare for the Chronomeister's arrival. He had the know-how, and a good arsenal of weapons. His engineering training had included not only the design and drafting of new parts and technological fixtures for production, but also the organization and management of production. He was familiar with time-and-motion studies and their techniques. The methods had been introduced to Ford by a Mr Taylor around 1915. This esteemed gentleman chose a well-trained giant of a man to unload a truck full of coal, and when the task was accomplished in four hours, Taylor decreed that every non-giant average Joe would have to do the same.

In this day and age, more sophisticated methods were employed. The chronomeisters of the world relied on, and preyed on, the pride of the worker, the determination to perform well, the refusal to let an unfinished car get by. When a worker fell behind, whether or not he was the cause, he had to walk longer distances to reach his components. He drifted toward the end of his zone, slipping into a hole, getting more and more behind, until he found himself entering the zone of the colleague whose work follows his. In such moments, pride injected the worker's veins with a relative of adrenaline—we might agree to call it pridealine—which almost instantaneously quickened his steps and accelerated the movements of his arms and hands. It caused the worker to shift into high gear, eliminating delays as he climbed out of the hole. These were the high-gear moments that widened a chronomeister's eyes. They caused him to press the buttons on his stopwatch like a maniac, separately recording each segment of the job, then adding up the fastest times and claiming—decreeing—that the job was doable, and therefore must be done, at that accelerated, emergency pace, because the stopwatch never lies. He measured an ideal time, not a real time, for each segment, leaving no room for error. The high-intensity two- or three-minute spurt thus became the new impossible standard to be maintained for ten hours. But that was no concern of the Chronomeister. He did his job. The operator, his supervisor, possibly his doctor, and the bureaucrats in the compensation office were left to deal with the disasters that followed as best they could.

You won't get me through my pride, Erik thought. Like anyone else, he was proud of his performance, of never letting an unfinished car go past him, not unless he really had to, on account of some technical problem beyond his control. But in this duel with the Chronomeister, he was determined to do the utmost to suppress his compensatory instincts. After eight months of performing the same sequence of moves, he could do them blindfolded and in a steady rhythm. To be on the safe side, he would count, like a metronome, to keep the timing of each segment as close to uniform as possible. If he couldn't complete the job, so be it. The guys down the line would understand. Everybody was aware of the upcoming match, and everybody was ready to contribute to the fight, to throw a punch or two, all the more since they believed Erik was the underdog, the odds stacked against him. The Chronomeister was considered all but unbeatable.

The supervisor, familiar with the Chronomeister's take-no-prisoners game, assigned two experienced guys to douse any fires generated by the shootout with Erik. He was worried. He had to let the Chronomeister do his job, but from afar he would watch Erik at work, hopefully averting disaster. He didn't want any impossible jobs on his line. He wasn't sure about Erik, though. He worked well, reliably, did a quality job, but was he a match for the tricky Chronomeister? Probably not. Even among supervisors, the Chronomeister had a dark reputation for victory. It was rumoured that his success rate was well over eighty percent.

I'll perform each movement consciously, rather than automatically, Erik told himself, *just how the Chronomeister's paperwork says.* Grab the long bolt in the right hand while the left one pushes a small rubber puck onto it, then grab the bigger rubber puck with the threaded metallic centre, push the bolt through the opening in the frame, catch the thread, and turn four half turns to equal two whole threads—eight seconds. Take two steps sideways, pull down the gun, tighten the three motor-mount bolts, one after another, then return the gun—fifteen seconds. Take three steps to the box of plastic washers and grab two washers, then take two steps sideways to the basket with the A-frames. Install the washers, remove the plastic cover protecting the lower ball joint, grab the A-frame—twelve seconds. Take three steps, place the A-frame on the frame, reach for two bolts and two nuts, push the bolts through the appropriate holes, hand-start threading the nuts, at least four half-turns to make sure the connection is okay. With both hands pull down the suspended horizontal gun that will hold the nuts and tighten both bolts at the same time. Position the gun sockets on the bolts and nuts and pull the trigger. After the bolts are tightened, release the gun and return it to the original position—twenty seconds. *On to the next car. Let him show me how he thinks he can save five seconds.*

While he waited for the Chronomeister to arrive at the scheduled time, Erik tried to get into what he called his judo frame of mind. During his undergraduate studies, he had taken judo lessons for four terms to obtain the required phys. ed. credits. It did him a great deal of good, mostly in the self-confidence department. It helped him remain cool whenever he got into a heated situation. He was no longer able to do most of the throws and pins, but he still recalled certain morsels of judo philosophy: with the right technique, you can defeat a much stronger opponent. Let him attack, use his momentum to disrupt his balance, and the takedown is yours. *Well,* thought Erik, *time to see if I can take down a bully by faking submissiveness.*

'Let's begin,' said the Chronomeister, having arranged his papers on a box just off the line. 'To start with, I want you to make just one half-turn instead of four when installing the F-mount. That should be sufficient, just to start the thread. It doesn't have to be sure-fire safe. Half a turn, understood?'

'Half a turn, yes, sir.'

Erik worked calmly, counting out his rhythm, blocking out everything but the job. He was surprised when the line stopped not even an hour later. He looked around to see who had pushed the stop button. Before he could locate the red light, he could hear the joyful yelling of Big Bernie: 'What a marvellous mess! What a beauty. You're doing awesome, brother!' It was he who'd shut down the line.

Bernie's nickname was fitting. He was a tall guy with wide shoulders, a bull neck, a beer barrel chest and arms as thick around as an average man's thighs. His passion and pleasure was polishing and driving his Harley-Davidson. He could have advanced to a better job long ago, having almost twenty years under his belt, but for some mysterious reason, he had stayed on the job that followed Erik's—spring compression. Erik guessed that this killer job kept Big Bernie in top physical shape and contributed to his big-bike manliness. Tough job for a tough guy. It required manipulating a huge, two-hundred-pound monster compressor, suspended from the rails above the line. After installing a coil-spring, he had to drag and hook this fixture to the frame, precisely position its one arm, then start the hydraulics that compressed the coil spring, allowing both upper and lower A-frames to be joined with a thick bolt and nut. Then the weighty monster had to be unhooked from the frame and pushed aside. After all those years at that job, Bernie's arms were really powerful. He had the strength to play with the monster as he wished. For example, when approaching the frame, he could let the monster ever so lightly touch the F-mount to reduce Erik's quarter turn on its thread to next to nothing. Then it was easy enough to exaggerate, just a bit, the shudder of the frame when the weight of the monster was released from it. The release produced a short, violent upward bounce of the front half of the frame, and … oops, there goes the F-mount. At least twenty rubber pucks cluttered the floor under Big Bernie's feet, and another fifteen could be seen under the box of coil springs. Now Big Bernie stood, his feet planted apart among the pucks, with hands on his hips like a god of indignation, and proclaimed his refusal to work on grounds of unsafe workplace. He might step on a puck, turn his ankle, maybe even trip and fall, and, in the worst-case scenario, let the monster slip out of his control and cause a much more serious injury.

Refusal to work on safety grounds never led to the standard stoppage of just a few seconds. Solving a safety problem required not only the supervisor, but also a general foreman and a Union rep. It took some time for them to arrive, then they had to discuss the nature of the threat and how they might eliminate it. The line could be down upwards of ten minutes. Erik sat down and rested. To work consciously, without tuning out and relying on muscle memory, was unusually hard, but he thought he had already scored a point. He was leading one to nothing.

The safety of Big Bernie's workstation was assured by adding a guy with a broom to keep the floor clean. Besides, a few minutes later, the Chronomeister changed his instruction: instead of one half turn, complete two turns of the F-mount bolt. The new instructions resulted in fewer pucks on the ground, though the problem hadn't been entirely eliminated. So the Chronomeister demanded only half a turn hand-start for the bolts and nuts that joined the A-frame to the car frame. That proved to be an even worse idea than fiddling with the F-mounts. Now and then a nut slipped off the bolt, the gun had to be returned to its starting position and a new nut installed. When the nut fell inside the frame it had to be extracted, or it would rattle around in there for the life of the car. A few times, the insufficiently hand-started nut was tightened across the thread. Each such case cost up to four minutes of downtime. Erik's gun had no reverse option, so a repairman had to be called in to release the faulty nut. Once, the torque of the gun made the nut shoot at least fifty feet away, just about causing another work refusal. One mess followed another. The rhythm of the job was completely out of kilter, but Erik didn't quicken his tempo one iota. To keep himself out of the hole, he had to let two cars go by without tightening the motor-mounts.

He was not surprised when, a few minutes later, the line stopped and the agitated supervisor appeared. How could Erik let a car go without its motor-mount tightened? Didn't he know that a job that takes him fifteen seconds when the bolts are easily accessible requires several minutes down the line, when the A-frame and the spring coil obstruct the repairman's access to the bolts? The supervisor had assigned a second repairman to the job, and still had to shut down the line. Couldn't Erik be more considerate, and think a little bit about the bigger picture? Erik just kept nodding. He was sticking to the priorities of his job. A-frames had to be completed at any cost, because the spring compression depended on them, and, since that required the monster compressor, it couldn't be done anywhere else. Motor-mounts and F-mounts *could* be done elsewhere, though with difficulty. The supervisor ordered Erik to finish the motor-mounts even if he had to stop the line to do so. Regardless of the Chronomeister. 'Yes, sir,' Erik answered cheerfully, far from offended. The supervisor might be giving him a hard time, but they were both on the same side. The supervisor was part of the Company hierarchy, and had to fight for his team, at least formally, though he knew well that if the Chronomeister succeeded in altering this job on his line, he would have to deal with the consequences for as much as a year, and, that, god forbid, might even endanger his position.

During this whole exchange, the Chronomeister pretended to be busy writing notes.

The line restarted. Erik wondered how long the Chronomeister would continue pushing the buttons on his stopwatch before he realized that computer games and reality occupied two very different worlds.

Ah, you grey theoretician, he thought, *welcome to the green trees of life. I can see that you've never worked on the line, or, if you ever did, you've long forgotten how it was. Just you wait. My little time bomb is ticking.*

A calamity, in the making for some time, was about to blow up in the Chronomeister's face. A-frames were delivered in wire boxes, called baskets, about five feet by four feet wide and four feet high. At the line, they were placed on hydraulic tables, so they could be lifted up and down, even slanted to make it easier for an operator to pick up the ten-pound frames without having to bend too much. The A-frames were fitted to a profiled plastic tray to prevent them from shifting during transport and forklifting. Six A-frames for one level, seven levels per basket. One basket supplied frames for about forty minutes' worth of work. Behind the hydraulic table, an empty basket stood on the floor waiting for empty trays to be deposited for return. The empty tray was lifted horizontally above the head and thrown, in a flat trajectory, towards the basket. With luck, it would glide along and land in the basket flat enough to slide to the bottom. But most times the tray didn't make it all the way down, either because it hadn't flown far enough or flat enough, or because it had flown too far. Most of the time it got stuck at odd angles against the sides of the basket. After the second or third improperly landed tray, the basket started looking like those three-dimensional X-shaped anti-tank obstacles. Subsequent trays slid over the top of the variously inclined planes and protruding corners and onto the floor behind the basket. If the Chronomeister hadn't been watching him, Erik would have been more careful in throwing the trays, and whenever the line was down for a few seconds, he would take a few steps around the table and release the stuck trays by hand so they could fill the basket full. That might take him fifteen or so seconds, not more than twenty. He had adjusted the trays that once, but the Chronomeister told him not to waste his time, and to just pay attention to the motor-mounts. *As you wish, boss.* Complying with the Chronomeister's orders, Erik let the trays litter the floor. He was almost sure that removal of the trays was accounted for in the time study, but not straightening the trays in the basket. That was Erik's *aha!* moment—when he saw exactly where the Chronomeister had made a mistake. A big mistake. *Pay attention, Monsieur Chronomeister. You're going to have to work much harder than this. Today I'm giving your homework an F. Straightening the plates is part of the job, sir, if you please.*

Every job entailed certain actions that didn't necessarily need to be completed for every single car, actions that needed to be performed only now and then, but which still had to be calculated into the time allotted for the job. Sometimes they were accounted for, sometimes they weren't, but Chronomeisters usually chose to ignore them, even deny them. Next time the repairmen stopped the line to deal with the motor-mounts, Erik grabbed a pencil and did a quick calculation on a piece of cardboard. Opening and closing of the basket—eight seconds, once every forty minutes. Lift the hydraulic table—three seconds, every six cars. Discard the empty trays—twelve seconds, every six cars. Straighten them in a basket—about fifteen seconds. A total of about thirty seconds every six cars. That would be, just off the top of the head, about five seconds per car. That equaled approximately ten percent of the total time—the ten percent that the Chronomeister hadn't taken into account. *Five seconds per car. I should ask him to remove some parts of my job, not add to it,* thought Erik. *I might just have to put this calculation on paper this evening, and give it to him as a parting gift, with copies to for the supervisor and the Union rep.*

The summoned forklift man refused to switch a full basket for an empty one. No less than four or five trays were on the floor blocking his access. Picking up empty trays from the floor was not in his job description. 'When you clean it up,' he said, 'call me back.' Once again, the supervisor had to save the day by ordering the guy with the broom sweeping up F-mount pucks to add picking up trays to his duties. 'Lovely mess,' Big Bernie delightedly proclaimed from time to time in his booming voice. The whole morning, the frame line had been moving as if it suffered from a severe hiccup. Several times the downtime was long enough to stop even the connected chassis line. The more experienced workers on that line concluded that the Chronomeister was wreaking havoc up the line. Less experienced workers enjoyed the havoc. It gave them time to stretch, straighten their backs, light a cigarette.

The Union rep came several times to make sure the Chronomeister wasn't exerting illegal pressure on Erik, wasn't punching below the belt. It looked like Erik was doing okay. Better than expected, to tell the truth. He stood nearby, watching both combatants, his eyes scanning the battleground for any hint of danger that would allow him to shut down the line, thus tripping up the Chronomeister once again. Professionally, he disliked both time studies and the agent of them, though he would not have liked to be in the Chronomeister's shoes, hated by the whole plant. How could he sleep at night, knowing how many injuries he had caused? Was he doing it for the money? Was it an ego trip? Well, it wasn't the Union rep's business.

Erik worked on with a smile. He knew that the Chronomeister had been thrown by all the stoppages. Now he just had to keep up the pressure. Surrender was imminent. Erik had plotted every move in the match, and he had a pretty good idea how the endgame would develop. If this were a boxing match, a referee would have stopped the fight by now, but as the only referee in this match was the Chronomeister himself, Erik would have to keep pinning him, squeezing the breath out of him. Opening a new basket meant missing an F-mount. Remove the tray and the motor-mount went undone. *I'm going to hit you with every second not spent directly on the line. I'm going to make you pay for your miscalculations, Mister Chronomeister,* thought Erik. *You're starting to look less self-assured as you bark your ever-changing orders. You're showing signs of oxygen deprivation. Enough for today? Pity, I was just starting to have fun. Next round tomorrow? My pleasure, sir.*

Back in his office after the first day of the time and motion study, the Chronomeister was obliged to admit that he hadn't made any progress. His stopwatch insisted that the subject moved lethargically. Erik offered no usable variability in his timing. He wouldn't speed up, no matter what. Had he no pride? How could he be provoked, derailed or panicked into moving faster? The Chronomeister worried that he had underestimated the subject. Despite his accent, he didn't seem stupid. His moves were rational, efficient, quick. No time to be found there. He hadn't been visibly sabotaging the study. He did what he was asked to do without argument. That F-mount stuff! Wasn't that a huge screw-up? Nothing in the database suggested that with spring compression the whole frame shudders so violently that even two turns of the screw were not enough. Well, mistakes happened, even to the best people....

On the following day, the Chronomeister took notes with increasing speed and decreasing legibility. He punched his stopwatch with such passion that it was a miracle he didn't crush it into a pancake. Maybe he *had* broken the thing. He reached for his spare stopwatch to make sure the original timepiece hadn't deceived him.

He knew—as Erik had forcefully reminded him—that creating efficiencies in one area of the line might create bigger inefficiencies elsewhere. Elimination of one operator might require two others to deal with the mess. Not to mention his perennial bugbear—the antagonism between speed and quality.

But though he was no longer an ambitious youngster, pursuing his job with ruthless passion, the Chronomeister wasn't used to giving up. Years of practice had made him a pragmatist. He was an expert at time-and-motion studies with twenty-five years of experience under his belt. He fondly remembered the early days when almost every job offered up moments when an operator might be caught reading a paper, or smoking, even playing poker or cribbage with his neighbour. There were so many reserves of time back then that he almost hadn't known which to target first. That was the golden era of time studies, and he had been king. Folks on the line trembled when he went by. What a time! He consoled himself that his current challenges were the result of his own successes in the past. His efforts had tightened the screw to the max.

Now, he watched Erik as if he were some exotic animal, with a mixture of awe and fear. He insisted on trying different numbers of turns on threads. It was as if his thinking had gotten stuck and was itself being tightened across the thread. Same results as on the previous day. Again and again. The Chronomeister had no other weapons. It dawned on him that he had chosen the wrong operator. This was no worker; this was a robot, a smart trickster android. It looked like game over.

'Thank you,' said the supervisor in a low voice. The Chronomeister gathered up all his paraphernalia and turned his back. This time he wasn't whistling. The guys down the line later claimed that he seemed agitated, was mumbling something to himself.

The Union rep was so perplexed that he slapped his forehead with enough force to almost knock himself over. 'Well, dumbass,' he said to Erik, 'you got the best of the so-called unbeatable big shot. Never seen anything like it. They should set you up as exhibit A in the Union hall, brother. Totally unique. A worker second to none. What's your secret?'

'I never try to convince anybody that his idea is foolish by arguing with him. Words achieve nothing. If he's an idiot, I prove it to him by bringing his idiotic idea to life. It is only when you illuminate the fallacies of his abstract thinking with the light of real life that he will understand how misguided he was. Oblige him, give him more than he asks for, now and then. Playfulness, my friend, turns work into fun, and fun produces joy. Just stand aside and watch him battle his own silly ideas.'

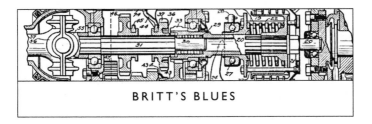

BRITT'S BLUES

Brittany was on probation, though not in the legal sense. Britt had never had anything to do with the courts of law. Rather, she was serving her three months of probation after being hired at Ford. She had coped well enough for the first eight weeks—she had endured all the aches, blisters, swollen fingers and hands, backaches, cramps, calluses, constant exhaustion, lost appetite, and nightmares that were part and parcel of the standard physical and mental adjustments to life on the assembly line. She had gotten used to the load, even finding time to relax a bit once in awhile. Recently, the line had almost seemed to slow, so she wasn't always having to chase her job down the line. She was starting to hope that she might be over the hump and would survive her probation. It would be over the week before Christmas. Four more weeks and she would be home free, a regular employee under the protection of the Union, unable to be fired without cause. She'd have a good, steady job—the best Christmas gift of all.

Britt had been very eager to get a job at Ford. She had completed high school and had lasted two terms at community college, but she had failed her exams and made the choice to drop out. After that, she'd held down a few jobs in the minimum wage category, and she'd gone through several boyfriends of minimum quality. It wasn't until the previous summer that life had begun to smile at her, and, touch wood, it would continue to do so. She'd met a very good-looking boy called Josh on the beach at Port Stanley. She'd smiled at him when she saw his eyes fixed—well, fixated—on the upper part of her bikini. His expression told her that he was imagining her without it. Laughing, she cut to the chase. 'I don't go topless,' she said. She wasn't bold enough to go around half-naked in public, but, if the circumstances were right, she could be persuaded to share the blessings of her beauty on occasion. After all, fine works of art or nature should not be secreted away in private collections *all* the time.

Since that encounter, she and Josh had been on about eighty dates, and a year ago, just before Christmas, they'd moved into an apartment together. Josh had a good job with the local branch of London Life. Britt was already hired by Ford and just waiting to be called in. Meanwhile, she sold coffee and Timbits at Tim Hortons, and, at home, made adventurous forays into the realm of culinary arts. Her relationship with Josh was like a dream—their connection was so strong that now and then both of them independently entertained nebulous thoughts about a wedding.

Eight weeks ago, in mid-September, Britt had been called in. She was lucky to have been assigned to a section of line three that had no real killer jobs. On line three, after the triple confluence of frame line, engine line, and line two, where parts were installed on a painted body, all the elements previously installed on separate lines had to be connected. Radiator hoses were attached on the engine line, but the radiator came with the body. Dashboard and steering column were part of the body, but the steering box was attached to the frame. Working here called for fast fingers and wrists, rather than a strong back. So, in her relatively decent job, Britt had made it from mid-September to late November—past the three-quarters mark of her probation. She was too sore to be truly happy as a lark, but the worst was now behind her. Or so she believed. Then her supervisor came and told her, somewhat apologetically, that he had to move her to a different job.

The regular operator on spare tire secure had gone down with appendicitis and was in hospital. He would be absent for at least three months. The guy with the misbehaving appendix had twelve years of seniority, so his was a good job, better than the one Britt had been doing, in fact. Her supervisor was positive that she could handle it, after the usual three days of training, of course. Britt just nodded. *Yes, sir!* She knew better than to object. She regularly repeated the basic rules for new hires: No absences. No complaints. No injuries. Also: The supervisor is untouchable and his word is law.

So Britt started a job that consisted of two sub-operations. First, she installed the plastic skirt separating the engine compartment from the wheel well, tightened the clips on the radiator hoses, and got the battery cables out of the way to help the guy five jobs down the line install the battery. It was a quick job, easily doable. Second, she secured the spare tire in the trunk. To do that, she had to grab an eight-inch-long spare tire tie-down bolt with a hook at the end, push it through the centre of the wheel rim to hook it up to the floor anchor in the trunk, then tighten the big nut with a gun. Not a bad job at all, and a dream job for a new hire—just so long as that person was at least five foot nine.

Britt, as it happened, was a couple inches short. She had no problem with the first part of her job working on the engine—the edge of the compartment was only slightly above her waist. But access to the spare tire was from the side, and she had to lean over the rear quarter panel because the tire was deposited flat, deep in the trunk, right behind the rear seats. Counting the eight inches of the line's elevation above the floor, the edge of the trunk was well over four feet high. Well, Britt could do the job, as long as she rose to her tiptoes at the critical moment of hooking the bolt. To do so, she had to rest her whole body on the rear quarter panel to use the whole length of her arm and fingers, right down to the last millimetre. The gun part was easier, because its length extended her arm by a foot or so.

Britt found the job uncomfortable, but manageable. She resolved to get used to it. No complaints. After her three days of training, once she was alone on the job, she ran through a gamut of experiments, trying out alternative ways of hooking the securing bolt. With her right hand, with her left hand. Leaning on the car sideways, leaning with her back. Nothing worked. Either her arm was too short or time was in short supply. She couldn't reach the tire from behind the trunk where its edge was lower, not without having the arms of an orangutan. Jumping into each trunk would take too much time, besides which, after some three hundred repetitions, her legs would give way. The only way to do the job seemed to involve a tiptoeing for a few steps, even though her safety boots did not lend themselves to balletic *en pointe*. Well, she would manage somehow. She would survive. After all, it was less than four weeks until the end of her probation.

Despite her resolve, a serious problem developed by the end of the first week. Britt's breasts began to ache from leaning her weight against the body of a car. Every time she leaned over the rear quarter panel, she felt a jolt of pain. During the second week, the pain became even more pronounced, and no wonder: during a single shift, she had to lean against the car no less than four hundred times. *I'm lucky we don't run ten-hour shifts now,* she consoled herself, trying to find some humour in the situation. At the end of each shift she kept repeating: *No complaints. No injuries. No complaints. No injuries. I have to bear the pain. I have to survive. Survive.* Then the pain stabilized somewhat, and she concluded that she might have a chance to get through the last few weeks of probation. After all, each new job initiates the novice into some kind of ache or sore spot, though Britt would never have guessed that, for her, the vulnerable spot would be mammary. In an automotive plant, of all places!

Josh found the situation upsetting and wanted her to go to Medical, but Britt convinced him it would be best for her to wait. She couldn't complain now, not without Union backing, and she wouldn't be in the Union until after probation. Only three more weeks, only fifteen more work days till December seventeenth.

Though it irritated every cell of his body, Josh promised her that he would not interfere.

A short time later, Britt went to see her family physician for a checkup, an appointment she had booked before she started at Ford. The doctor was deeply concerned. Britt's chest displayed colours ranging from a prevalent blueberry blue to the green of conifers and meadows to highlights of mustard yellow. Of course, he inquired about the origins of such an affliction. Britt explained the physical demands of her job on the line, adding that she had just a little over two weeks to go, after which she might be able to request a different job. The doctor just nodded. From a medical standpoint, there was not much he could do. Certain anaesthetics might help a little, but they were only topical and would not go deep enough to provide real relief. She should visit him again immediately, he said, if the problem grew worse or if inflammation appeared. He wished her good luck for the final two weeks of her probation.

When he arrived home, the good doctor happened to describe the unusual case to his wife. No one ever found out how, exactly, word of Britt's bruising began to spread, but it did, and the story took on a life of its own. Three days later there was a knock at the door of Britt's and Josh's apartment. Britt had just returned from work. After a quick shower, she was relaxing with her feet up, sipping a beer. Josh answered the door.

The lady standing there identified herself as a volunteer with a shelter for battered women, and demanded to speak to Britt. Once inside, she assured Britt that the door of the shelter was always open to her, and that she shouldn't hesitate to come 'if this brute of yours starts in beating you about the breasts again.' Britt was so flabbergasted that she just listened, mouth agape, shaking her head. But the woman carried on doggedly. 'We can give you protection, you know. We can help you get a restraining order against him. You could choose to charge him in a court of law—your injuries qualify as bodily harm, you know.'

Finally, Britt caught her breath and managed to cut into the lady's torrential monologue. She assured her that the state of her breasts had absolutely nothing to do with her boyfriend, that the injuries had a completely different source, and, anyway, that was nobody's business but her own.

'My poor child,' the lady exclaimed, 'you're living in denial! You suppress the reality because it's unbearable. It often happens that an abused woman stands behind her brute of an assaulter, yes, fosters illusions about his true nature, even excuses his excesses. We can help with all of this. We employ a psychologist qualified to analyze your case and help you understand the truth of the situation.'

Britt stared at the lady as if she was an apparition, a spook, a ghost. She was a bit afraid of her, but then she realized that the idea was to separate her from her Josh and she found her words. She stated categorically that Josh hadn't touched her breasts for the last two weeks, and that if he *were* to do so in some unwanted manner, she knew where the shelter was and wouldn't hesitate to call upon their assistance. She thanked the woman for her concern, but now it was time she got the hell out of here! Only after this outburst was she able to in push the lady out into the hallway and lock the door. Britt finished her beer in one long pull, shuddered with disgust at the visitor's opinion of Josh, and opened another bottle. Her day had been spoiled.

During a long conversation with Josh, she shared her fears that the well-meaning lady might, with the best intentions, unwittingly trigger an avalanche of attention involving the police and the courts, possibly ending with the loss of the job at Ford, and even, perish the thought, driving a serious wedge between Britt and Josh. Britt couldn't fall asleep for a long time. Who had alerted that lady? How had she tracked down Britt's address? It couldn't be the doctor; he was bound by privacy rules. Was it the doctor's receptionist who started all this? The whole next day at work she kept repeating the number she had written in lipstick on the anteroom mirror to cheer herself up: the number seven. *Only seven more days.... Only seven more, ouch, more days.... Only seven....*

Two days later, her suspicions proved to be well founded. She and Josh were just sitting down to dinner—takeout from Domino's Pizza, because Britt was too exhausted to stand at the stove after the shift, and Josh needed a break from cooking—when they heard an energetic pounding at the door. Josh got up to answer it, saying, 'If it's that witch again, I'm going to slam the door in her face! Then I'll open it again and kick her down the stairs.' But it wasn't her. It was a different woman, this one from social services at City Hall, come to investigate a case of domestic violence that had been reported. She warned Josh that if he did not allow her to enter the apartment, she would be returning with a police officer. So Josh ground his teeth and stepped aside and let her in. All three sat at the kitchen table while the woman filled out some forms. Her questions were for Britt alone; she had nothing but angry looks for Josh, though he remained completely silent. Britt assured the woman that her life with Josh was very harmonious and happy, even exemplary, and that she needed no help or intervention from social services. In the end, to stop the insistent woman, she confided that the state of her breasts was an unfortunate and unforeseen consequence of her work, but that she was not going to provide any further details. 'Let this go,' she warned the woman. 'If you don't leave me alone, I may well end up becoming your client—as a welfare recipient. In a week, I'll be able to explain my predicament to you, or anybody, but, for the time being, goodbye.'

'What a scandal!' the woman exclaimed. 'So the employer is the guilty party. We can't let such abuse pass unnoticed. Poor girl, women have to fight such brutality and injustice. If you won't do it, others will!' She shouted her last words from the stairs, because Britt's patience had run out and she had ordered the visitor out in no uncertain terms.

The next two days went by quietly. The weekend was filled with

Christmas season activities: shopping, decorating the tree, putting up the Christmas lights, vacuuming the whole apartment. While Josh did all this, Britt successfully attempted two batches of Christmas cookies, which she could mostly do while sitting. On Monday afternoon, as she left for her night shift, she looked at the number five on the mirror and whispered to herself: *Five shifts! I can survive five shifts with my hands tied behind my back.*

When Josh was unlocking the door on the way from work the next day, he could hear the phone ring inside the apartment. He didn't manage to pick it up in time, but another call came twenty minutes later. Josh answered. It was a reporter. She told him that she was writing an article about what she believed to be less-than-welcoming behaviour towards some of the female employees at the local factory, and that she would love to interview Britt. Such a serious issue had to be brought to public attention and the culprits held accountable, in fact pilloried. 'My article is almost done,' she told Josh cheerfully. 'I need just a few colourful details to give it the flavour of real life. When can I speak to Britt?'

'Never!' Josh slammed down the receiver. He sat at the kitchen table and fought off alternating bouts of desperation and rage. 'Damn these bitches! They're going to push their agenda even if it costs Britt her job! Why in hell do these busybodies insist on saving her against all reason, against her own will, even against her own interests?

Josh was justifiably terrified by the disaster looming over them. If the article were published, Britt would never succeed in convincing anybody that she wasn't behind it. She'd be fired from Ford, even after probation, even if she belonged to the Union. She'd never be able to get another factory job in this city. Josh would be painted in this whole mess as a brute and a ruffian, a label that would stick, even if it were exposed as pure fantasy, and proven wrong again and again. He and Britt might have to leave St. Thomas altogether, maybe move to London, even Toronto, just to escape the consequences of these so-called do-gooders. In the end, he smashed the table with his fist, stood up, and spoke in a low, determined voice. 'Sorry, Britt, I promised you I'd stay out of your struggle, but it's time for me to join in. I have to take a chance. I don't see any other way to fend off this mega-catastrophe.'

He drove to the Ford plant. He needed to ask how to get through the gate, but that didn't take more than a couple of minutes. The guard let him through the guardhouse at the gate, then showed him how to find the Union offices. The young Union rep on duty, after hearing a little of what was afoot, brought in an older and more senior colleague, a heavily built, greying, slow-talking chap. He introduced himself as a member of the Union leadership in the plant, and offered his help. Josh told him the whole story of Britt being assigned her current job, its unexpected consequences, her fear of telling anybody before being a Union member, and the threat of very bad publicity for both her and Ford that was looming now. 'Hum, hum,' said the Union rep thoughtfully, 'no porridge is eaten as hot as it's cooked … and so on.' Of course, the Union will support Britt, he concluded. Those four remaining days were nothing, a mere formality. The Union doesn't like muckraking articles about the plant written by journalists with nothing better to do. The Union had been fighting for women to be welcomed and treated fairly in the plant, and was proud of what had been achieved. He would take care of Britt's case himself. No formal complaint. That might be unwise. After all, there is a collective agreement that sanctions firing within the probation period, and the Union must abide by it. No, the solution would have to be arrived at by negotiations in good faith. Person to person. Who should do it? The regular Union rep of Britt's line was on the warpath with the supervisor as a result of everyday skirmishes. The supervisor would oppose him on principle, so, tactically, the youngster wouldn't be the right choice. No, he, himself, would personally visit the supervisor. Even though supervisors side with the Company, they are people too, and sometimes they think and behave in a human way. 'You know, he's a man. It probably didn't cross his mind that Britt's job might give her boob problems. Well, the whole thing should be solvable with a few good words.'

Ever since returning home, right up until half an hour past midnight, Josh couldn't help marching from the living room to the bedroom, from the bedroom to the bathroom, from the bathroom to the kitchen, over and over again, fifty times, a hundred times. Should he or should he not have interfered? How would it all end? Sometimes he was sure that he and Britt were going to have to move to Toronto, if not Vancouver, to escape all the gossip. Sometimes he allowed himself to hope that Britt would be allowed to keep her dream job. She certainly deserved it, having won it against great odds. For the whole three months, ninety days, day after day, shift after shift, she'd given a heroic performance.

The key rattled in the lock, the door opened. One look into Britt's face melted all of Josh's tension. She was buoyant, radiant, in a laughing mood. She buried herself in her easy chair and stretched out her legs on the coffee table while Josh brought her a beer.

'What a night,' she exclaimed. 'You wouldn't believe it! Shortly after dinner, a big, heavy-set, unfamiliar guy came to our line. He stood in the aisle, watched me to do my job for a while, then nodded and walked away. A short time later I saw him in a discussion with my supervisor. Both were gesticulating, and, probably because their hands were making rounded gestures, I guessed they were talking about me. About twenty minutes later the supervisor came over. He looked kind of ill at ease. His eyes kept landing on my breasts. Then he blurted, 'Sorry, Britt, I didn't know, I had no idea. Starting tomorrow, you go back to your old job. You had no problems there, did you?' When he said that, I fell into a fit of uncontrollable laughter. I was bent double. I missed two cars. I was laughing like crazy, couldn't stop. I had an impulse to hug the guy, but it flashed through my mind that I wouldn't be able to do that without crying 'ouch, ouch, ouch,' and I laughed some more. So, it's done! I'm through the rapids! Only four more days of probation, and it'll be on my old job. Isn't that marvelous? Did you ever expect such an ending? Could you bring me another beer, please?'

The case of the social worker was shelved. The Union had numerous working and personal contacts with social services at City Hall, and it was easy to explain that no brutality had transpired, either in the bedroom or on the assembly line, that the whole case sprang from a simple misunderstanding. The journalist was invited to the plant to give her the opportunity to verify her information on the spot, and in the end no article appeared, because the basic premise had been completely undercut.

Ten days later, a full-fledged employee of Ford and a Union member, Britt shared Merry Christmas wishes with all her colleagues as they left after their shift for twelve days of holidays. She shook her supervisor's hand and wished him a really wonderful Christmas. Then she added: 'I owe you something,' and gave him a big hug. She could do it now.

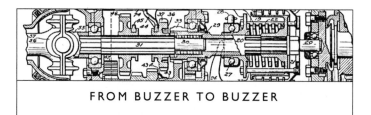

FROM BUZZER TO BUZZER

'Where do you think you're going?' Rudi's supervisor, Benny, blocked his way, his arms crossed.

'What a stupid question, Benny! Home, of course.'

'Have you heard the buzzer? I haven't.'

'It's coming in less than a minute. I finished my work. I'm going home.'

'This constitutes unauthorized leave from your work station,' said Benny stiffly. 'We'll be talking about it tomorrow.'

Rudi just shrugged his shoulders, gave a little thought to where the supervisor could kiss him, and kept on marching towards the locker room without a backwards glance. This wannabe dictator was beginning to get on his nerves. Rumour had it that Benny was some relation—a nephew or son-in-law or something—of a big shot, that he spent time among the white shirts, and that he had ambitions to climb the ranks. He wanted to be a supervisor so he could manage people, order them around, and after completing the required course, he'd been assigned to the engine line about three weeks ago. Since then he'd been annoying the workers on his line, pestering them when they didn't do their jobs to his standards.

Rudi was a seasoned Fordmate. At twenty, he had turned his former business repairing lawnmowers and forging ornamental railings into a weekend hobby, and he got himself hired on at Ford to secure a better future for his family. He spent twenty-two years in the plant, serving some time on the frame line, and the last sixteen years on the engine line, working through a dozen jobs there. Now he could perform them all to the highest standard. Those acquired skills had granted him the esteemed job classification of utility man. He was important, a worker highly valued, the right man for many jobs. Gifted with extraordinarily deft hands, he had an intuitive understanding of all things mechanical. He could speak the language of metal.

Having mastered so many jobs, Rudi could cover any of them at a moment's notice, which offered his supervisor great flexibility. Absenteeism was the bugaboo of every supervisor. There were two solutions. Temporarily swapping in a utility man was best. Rudi could take over installing radiator hoses if the regular guy had the runs and needed an extra bathroom break, or needed to pick up a painkiller at Medical when his tendinitis flared up. He could double as a repairman. He could do just about any job when the regular operator decided to take in a ball game in the comfort of his own home, rather than spend Friday evening sweating on the line. Another option was to divide a job into two separate processes, borrow two workers from other lines, and give them ten minutes of training before leaving them to it. It was more costly for the supervisor, but sometimes it was the only choice. At the beginning of a shift, it was quite common for phones to ring constantly as supervisors searched for lines with a surplus from which to borrow operators for the day. The utility man would train them, after which he could lead an easy life. When everything ran smoothly, he could even sit down and relax. But there were jobs that couldn't be divided, or else they required more intensive training in handling a specific gun or fixture, or reading teletype and choosing the right component to be installed. Such responsibilities could not be entrusted to temporary help borrowed from other lines. The jobs cursed with most absences were, of course, the killer jobs. In them, the utility man had to weather a hard shift. Rudi didn't mind. He found ways of enjoying every task. He liked going from job to job. The variety kept him from getting bored with the usual routine.

Most of his supervisors appreciated the fact that Rudi was able to fill in anywhere, at any time, but also that he didn't insist on working. Though it was a rare occurrence, it sometimes happened that everybody was present and on the job—no absences—and the supervisor had to send one or two surplus people home. Rudi often volunteered so he could spend the day working on some pet project, like hand-shaping a fifteenth-century suit of armour. Flexibility made the utility man a treasure for his supervisor. Such a treasure was to be appreciated—and treated as such.

Experienced supervisors, those well schooled by the endless whimsies thrown at them by the line, knew this well. Benny didn't. For one thing, he was as green as they come and, for another, he was a natural paper-pusher. During his supervisor's course, he had studied diligently—even beyond the curriculum. Besides attending the lectures, he had read through and memorized just about every manual, every regulation, every nuance of standard operating procedure. He believed in the efficacy of the theoretical, in the power of the printed word. Benny didn't like moving into unregulated territory, didn't like to improvise. The manuals offered him a shred of security in the turbulent life of a supervisor. But uncompromising application of all his hard-won knowledge soon aroused in his subordinates a significant level of aversion.

The tension between Benny and the guys on the line made Rudi nervous. As an old-timer, he felt a certain amount of responsibility for the line. Extensive experience often made a utility man into an unofficial right-hand man or advisor to his supervisor. In fact, not so long ago, the general foreman had offered Rudi the position Benny now enjoyed, provided he go through the supervisor's course. Rudi declined. He didn't want to manage people, and hated the very idea of paperwork.

Rudi had served under a number of supervisors over the years, so he knew with absolute certainty that any supervisor who managed to antagonize his workers on a regular basis quickly learned that his days were numbered. So, the day after his slightly early departure from work, Rudi again threw a 'see ya' over his shoulder and kept walking to the locker-room. Same on the third day. On the fourth day, before his shift, he was summoned to Benny's portable office. There, he was lectured about abandoning his workstation without authorization for three days straight. Only at the buzzer, and not a second sooner, could he leave the plant and go home. Having spent an easy shift as additional repairman—there'd recently been an unusually high need for repair—Rudi was in a good mood, so rather than take offense, he calmly explained to Benny that, whenever the job permitted, everybody on the line sped up just before the end of shift, so as to move one or even two extra cars up the line. That's how it was done. That's how it had *always* been done. The work was completed a minute or two before the buzzer, and everyone went home.

Benny slammed his desk with a fist. 'That is completely unacceptable!' he shouted. 'You work for me. I'm paying you to work from three thirty to twelve midnight. Twelve zero zero. Not eleven fifty-eight. That's what work and wages regulations stipulate. That's what is expected of you.'

Rudi looked at him without expression, and without a hint of comprehension. Here was a new variant of ignorance he hadn't yet encountered on the line. He tried again. 'But my work is all done, just as if I stayed until twelve zero zero. Isn't that what counts?'

'What counts is that you are physically present at your workstation right up to the buzzer goes off at twelve zero zero.'

Rudi finally understood that he was not dealing with a regular, sensible Ford supervisor. He said so. 'Look Benny, don't be a bureaucratic jackass. S.O.P.s are one thing, but life on the line is quite another. Everybody bends the regulations just a bit, adjusting for circumstances on the job. It makes life here a touch more pleasant. That includes leaving a couple of minutes of early, especially when the work we're supposed to do is done. Robots may work in the body shop, but if our jobs on the line could have been automated, it would have been done a long time ago. You might as well look the other way, just like everyone else. You are supervising people, not robots.'

Benny didn't answer. He dismissed Rudi with a wave of his hand, but he was pissed off. Nobody was going to lecture *him* about his managerial skills, certainly no subordinate.

At the end of that shift, he waited in view of Rudi's workstation. He watched, fuming, as the utility man left his station the usual minute or so early. He opened his mouth to protest, but Rudi spoke first.

'Go to hell, Benny,' he said as he passed. Then, 'See ya.' At that very moment, the buzzer sounded, so Rudi was no longer his underling.

For the rest of the week Rudi stayed out of Benny's way, not talking to him except about matters strictly related to work. He was summoned to the office again, and this time was given an official warning. The Union rep, whose presence was required for any disciplinary action, was confused by the absurdity of the situation. After the session, he asked Rudi what kind of a moron Benny was. Should the Union put some heat on him?

'Leave him to me,' Rudi said. 'Just keep your eye on developments. Keep some records so we can argue the case later, if necessary. He's young, green, ambitious, and ignorant. I'll give him one more chance. If he refuses to take it, then the gloves are off.'

The time bomb started ticking. That following Thursday, while looking at his paycheque, Rudi discovered he'd been paid for 39.8 hours though, as always, he had done forty hours' worth of work. He stood in the doorway of Benny's little office to confront him about the discrepancy and received a lecture. 'A two-minute premature departure per day times five days makes ten minutes, rounded off from twelve. You weren't working for those ten minutes. I don't have to pay you for time you won't work. If you keep violating the rules, you'll force me to suspend you for a day. Don't play with me, boy.' Rudi glared at his supervisor with visceral contempt. His face must have been quite legible, because Benny bellowed: 'From buzzer to buzzer!' before rising abruptly and slamming the door in Rudi's face, so forcefully that he almost unhinged it.

'As you wish,' Rudi growled at the closed door. 'Seven zero zero until three three zero—the morning shift, according to the regulations. You call for exactitude, you'll get exactitude.' He dropped one of his work gloves in front of Benny's door. Rudi had thrown down the gauntlet.

Monday morning ushered in two weeks of morning shifts. Mondays, coming as they did right after a weekend, were often burdened by absences—not as many absences as Fridays, but still a considerable number. Rudi arrived at work at a quarter to seven, as usual, and sat at a picnic table to enjoy his coffee. He wore headphones. In a few minutes, Benny appeared and told him he'd be covering starters for the morning. Jerry had a dental appointment, wouldn't be in before eleven. Rudi's face remained blank. He gave no indication that he'd heard the instruction. His hands moved as if he were conducting the music blaring out of his headphones. He was so obviously ignoring Benny that the supervisor couldn't fail to notice. He tried again. 'Do you hear me?' he bellowed. 'Today, until eleven, you're on starters!' He tried to remove Rudi's headphones, but now Rudi spoke in a singsong: 'Rudi not here, Rudi come at seven.' Benny kept on shouting, but Rudi didn't react. Only when the buzzer sounded and the lines began moving did he remove his headphones and sweetly ask, 'You were saying?'

'To starters, you prick! On the double!'

'Yes, sir.' Rudi went to the metal cabinet to pick up a pair of gloves, then slowly made his way to the workstation where starters were installed. In the meantime, three cars went down the line without starters, and because the repairman had only one starter on his shelf, he had to shut down the line to go get the other two. Of course, that attracted the attention of the general foreman. He was allergic to line stoppages. The extent of his allergy could be measured by the decibels of his vocalizations; he yelled in frustration louder than any drill sergeant ever did.

The same farce repeated itself on Tuesday and Wednesday. Rudi listened to music until the buzzer, and if he answered Benny at all, it was with the same singsong: 'Rudi not here, Rudi come at seven.' That phrase made Benny all but foam at the mouth because he had no idea what to do about it, what the rules authorized him to do. It was impossible to tell his utility man, before seven o'clock, where he was needed for the day, and that meant the line was always shut down for at least two, and more likely four minutes. Every shutdown put penalty points to Benny's name in the general foreman's notebook. Even the repairman had to stop the line more often than usual because, for some reason, there were more repairs coming at him than he could handle.

Thursday morning, before the shift, the general foreman called Benny to account for the unacceptable downtime. 'My dear associate,' he began in a friendly tone. 'Rules and regulations are just a framework that requires creative application. Do you know the biggest asset of any supervisor? People skills. Technical knowledge is all well and good, troubleshooting is necessary of course, and learning S.O.P.s chapter and verse will help you advance, but those aren't everything. No, it's people skills that make a good supervisor! Applying those skills eliminates half of the potential calamities you might face. Either you prevent them completely, or your workers will deal with them because they don't want to cause you trouble. Don't be looking for a fight with your subordinates. A friendly approach and a bit of humour can work miracles.' He sighed and shook his head sadly. 'Maybe it would have been better to let you work your way up to supervisor, after ten or so years on the line. That would teach you far more about management than all those manuals ever could. I advise you, I beg you, do not antagonize your people. There'll be twenty-five of them against one of you, and they can get you into disasters you can't even imagine. They can do it with smiling faces and without leaving a lick of proof. I will send you to work on the line for a while if I must. Don't tempt me.'

The dressing down shook Benny to the core. The combat between Benny and Rudi was common knowledge and inventing innocuous tricks to make Benny see red had become a popular pastime on the engine line. Others had been toying with him like matadors toyed with a rampaging bull. The line was shutting down with increasing frequency, and Benny became more and more prone to bouts of helplessness, even panic. Now he had the threat of the general foreman hanging over his head. He studied the manuals ever more diligently, but found no answers in them, nothing about 'people'. He slept poorly. On Friday morning, he had a terrible headache and bloodshot eyes.

That morning, Rudi sat at a picnic table, as usual, a cup of coffee in hand. Benny charged in with the force of a tornado. Today he needed Rudi to cover a job that couldn't be doubled up: coupling engine with transmission. There were about ten different types of transmissions, and the right one had to be selected by consulting the teletype, picking it up with a hoist, bringing it to the engine, hooking them together and securing the connection with several bolts. It was a job that called for experience, skill, and, above all, responsibility. It was job number two, done near the beginning of the line, right after engine selection and pickup. Without it, the engine couldn't progress down the line since the coupling couldn't be performed anywhere else. Only Rudi could do it. Today, everything depended on Rudi, and the utility man revelled in his indispensability. Benny was at once wild and imploring. He might have been willing to get down on his knees and beg, but his utility man just kept saying, 'Rudi not here, Rudi come at seven.'

Just before the buzzer, Benny was summoned back to his office to answer the phone. He wasn't out until three minutes after seven. Of course, when he emerged, the line was down.

Rudi smiled at Benny and asked, 'What'll it be today, boss?'

Benny almost grabbed Rudi by the throat, but managed to contain the urge. 'Transmissions!' he barked. 'On the double!'

'Yes, sir,' said Rudi. In his usual leisurely way, he headed to the cabinet to pick up his gloves. He chose two pairs with leather palms and sauntered off to the beginning of the line. It was going to take him two minutes to get there, thought Benny, and another minute to finish the first coupling.

At that very moment, the general foreman's voice came yelling into his walkie-talkie: 'Why is your damned line down again?'

Benny snapped. With a few quick steps, he reached Rudi, laid both hands on his shoulders and pushed him to make him walk faster. But rather than speed up, Rudi stopped dead. Benny's momentum carried his knee into Rudi's lower back. Rudi cried out and collapsed to the floor. Workers gathered around him while he moaned in apparent pain. After a dramatic pause, he said he was going to have to go to Medical immediately. He asked for a Union rep to be summoned because he was refusing to work on the grounds that his workplace was not safe. He would refuse to work as long as unsafe conditions persisted. The general foreman sped in on his three-wheeler. His mouth twitched with just the hint of a smile when he found Rudi sprawled on the ground, an ashen-faced Benny hovering over him. The gathered workers began to chant, 'Heads are gonna roll, heads are gonna roll.' There was a kind of triumph in their voices, reminiscent of the jeering crowds in Paris when Marie Antoinette and Robespierre were dragged to the guillotine. 'Heads are gonna roll.' The words rippled down the line, an augury of good news ahead.

With great effort, Rudi managed to sit up. He massaged his lower back and asked a pale Benny: 'Could you tell me, please, what the regulations have to say about the consequences of physically attacking a fellow worker or subordinate? Is it not grounds for immediate dismissal?' Then he closed his eyes to emphasize his suffering.

The general foreman quickly evaluated the situation, ungently elbowed Benny aside, and bent down to Rudi. For his ears only, he said, 'Look, pal, enough is enough. I won't put up with this malicious compliance crap any longer. You don't need Medical. Yeah, you're within your rights to go, and you could keep the line down for another twenty minutes if you really wanted to, but there's already been too much downtime. Don't do it, man. Get up and get to those transmissions so we can finally get the damn line going. If you go right now, I'll take care of everything with your Union rep and I will personally guarantee that the troublesome element you've encountered here will be removed from the line. So what do you say? Will we start the line?' Rudi stood, and three minutes later the line started moving.

Half an hour later, the general foreman and the Union rep finished questioning the witnesses, and had, according to protocol, a written report on the incident. Benny was demoted on the spot. With trembling hands, he surrendered his walkie-talkie and supervisor's jacket. He looked around in vague disbelief, as if punchdrunk. With head hung low, he slowly walked away from what was once his line. To the office? To the parking lot? Maybe to hell. His retreat was accompanied by a cheerful chorus—'Head's are gonna roll, heads are gonna roll'—until Rudi, the hero at the centre of all the attention, who could now afford to be magnanimous, raised his arms. With a few graceful gestures, as if conducting an orchestra, he modulated the chant from forte to piano to pianissimo, to silence.

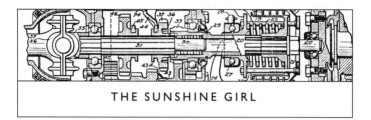

THE SUNSHINE GIRL

Ever since morning a disquieting rumour had drifted from one line to another, like the shadow of a cloud creeping between the sun and the earth and blocking the sunshine. The rumour was that all photos of scantily clad girls, maidens, ladies, damsels, and women were about to be banned from the workplace.

This creeping shadow made Sandy jittery. His daily routine, upon arrival at work, involved drinking a cup of coffee and leafing through the *Toronto Sun*. Three pages before the end of the paper, a full-page color photo of the 'Sunshine Girl' bid him good morning. The paper featured a different Sunshine Girl every day. Her photo used to be on page three, but for some reason it was moved to the back pages. Maybe to illustrate the saying 'all's well that ends well', or 'save the best for last'. Most of the time, the Sunshine Girl wore a swimsuit, but sometimes she had on a T-shirt and shorts. Occasionally she sported a Blue Jays or Maple Leafs jersey, according to her fancy, or to that of the photographer. A caption offered three or four lines of information about the girl: her first name, her studies at a community college to become a dental technician or whatever, whether her favourite activities included reading romance novels and going to the movies, or camping in the summer and skating in winter. Those lines, along with the likeness of the Sunshine Girl, offered Sandy a modicum of inspiration, a slight lift in mood. The photo was no marvel of photographic art nor was it an example of outstanding printing quality, so its erotic qualities were practically nil. It was a routine picture in a newspaper. He would snip out the picture, pin it above his workstation, and engage in conversation with the Sunshine Girl throughout the day. Taking clues from the caption, he would imagine what kind of girl she might be, what thoughts might preoccupy her mind, what they might talk about if they went skating, how to go about inviting her for dinner, what her favourite meal might be, whether she might top off her dinner with dessert. That kind of thing. Sandy was no teenager. He was pushing forty. Fifteen years on the line had allowed him to develop and refine ways of keeping himself entertained while working. He knew how to control his imagination, so he never became its victim. Prompted by the photo of the day, he invented an endless variety of scenarios. His daily reveries never ended in bed—they were not of the salacious variety—but with the buzzer signaling the end of his shift. Another workday successfully survived, thanks to his Sunshine Sweetie.

Beside talking to the Sunshine Girl, Sandy had discovered another solar pleasure to enjoy on the line. Generally, the plant was well fortified against nature. You could spend the whole day inside, never knowing that, in the outside world, thunderstorms had alternated with shockingly blue skies, or that a blizzard had dumped ten inches of snow on the parking lot. The weak spots in the fortifications were six-foot-wide openings in the flat roof, through which massive ventilators sucked in fresh air to supply the whole plant. When there were no clouds outside, sunshine snuck past the fans and painted intense rectangles of light that slowly moved across the floor in concert with the sun as it moved across the sky. It was by no means ever dark inside the plant, but the brightness of sunlight made even the strongest artificial lighting seem dim and muted as candlelight. For Sandy, this shaft of sunlight, this moving island of brightness, signified an infiltration of nature into the artificial, technological insanity of the assembly plant. All winter, he looked forward to those rays of sunshine, and from late April until midsummer, when the sun rose high in the sky, he delighted in watching the colourful cars floating, one after the other, through the sunshine. If he was lucky, the miracle could last as long as two hours.

Sandy was blessed to have a decent job on a decent line. It had taken him eleven years on various killer jobs, half-killer jobs, and almost-decent jobs on the frame line, and then on line one, to climb the seniority ladder to the line called trim. His job involved installing the mechanisms for cranking the driver-side window up and down. Suspended in huge yellow jaws, the cars on this line floated along in the air, about a foot above the floor, so that a worker needn't stretch or bend too much. There were reasonable gaps between the cars, and the whole line had an air of roominess and light, unlike, say, the crowded frame line. His counterpart on the passenger side, Jenny, had been hired about two years ago. She was thirty-something, about halfway between plain and pretty. Rumour had it that she was a really good soccer player and she was easygoing and curious about how things worked in the plant. Early on, she had indicated a willingness to talk to Sandy while they worked, but Sandy had remained taciturn at first. It was nothing personal—it was just that his sense of fair play had been offended. It had taken him twelve years to get this job, and she got it right off the bat. The whole process of hiring and deploying women in the last years had rubbed him the wrong way. The introduction of women on the line interfered with the whole seniority system. New hires are supposed to be assigned to the worst jobs, to be replaced after a year or two by fresh new hires, so a person could slowly but steadily rise to better and better jobs. Newly hired women blocked that path by sliding into jobs at the eight- to twelve-year level. Strain injuries from repetitive jobs were multiplying. But over time Sandy came to see that Jenny did a good, honest day's work, and his resentment gave way to tentative cordiality and the occasional smile or short conversation. He was relaxed in his job, quite content on his line.

But then the rumour went round that the white shirts wanted

to outlaw his Sunshine Girl. His first reaction was outrage, but he calmed when he reminded himself that nobody had ever objected to his pictures. Sunshine Girls were never naked like the women in *Playboy*. Most posed in bikinis, and revealed nothing more than might be seen on the beach. The pictures were published in a newspaper, a virtual guarantee that they didn't violate any sense of public decency. The *Toronto Sun* was a serious, respected paper, after all, so everything should be safe on that score. Maybe the prohibition only referred to those photographs of girls who couldn't afford swimsuits, or who'd forgotten their bikinis at home before heading out to meet a photographer from *Penthouse*.

But his hopes were dashed when Archie, his Union rep, appeared during his regular rounds shortly before noon. After the usual how-are-you-I'm-fine exchange, he pointed to the photo and said: 'Today is the last day for that.'

'You mean I'm not allowed to read the *Sun*?'

'Of course, you can read it. You just can't cut out that photograph and display it here.'

'What kind of idiot came up with such rubbish?' Sandy protested, pausing in his work.

'It came from above. I mean, really the highest above. The Union's leadership issued the regulation jointly with the Company.'

For a while Sandy worked faster, to keep from falling behind and sliding into a hole. 'So, some white-shirt at corporate decreed the end of the Sunshine Girl?'

'Well, not quite. You can have her,' Archie explained, 'you just can't display her for everybody to see. She can't be standing up; she has to be horizontal, on her back, so to speak.'

'You've got a dirty mind,' Sandy shouted after the retreating back of his Union rep. His blood pressure rose with suspicion that his happy days on the line were over. Without the company of those Sunshine Girls, his eight- to ten-hour shifts would be endless. And he was affronted by Archie's jocular insinuation. Flat on her back?

Had he never talked to a woman? In a proper conversation, you looked into her eyes and she looked into yours. Whether the conversation took place while walking, or sitting on a park bench, or even ice skating, she stood up—she was vertical, to use Union parlance. When talk progresses to lying down, both man and woman can usually manage without words.

Sandy knew that the Company's main priority was productivity. But it had been established beyond reasonable doubt that the plant experienced the least downtime and built the best quality cars during the World Series and the Stanley Cup Finals. At such times, every other worker on the line had his eyes glued to a portable TV and worked on total autopilot. For those few hours, everybody performed mindlessly, flawlessly, transformed into the ideal worker. So why would the Company suddenly object to a few unobjectionable pictures that inspired innocent daydreams and better quality work?

And the Union! The Union brass should know how much workers valued the rare moments when the mind detached itself from the line and floated away like a hot-air balloon. They should know that pissing off their membership constituted poor motivational strategy. Who knew what they were thinking when they devised this regulation. He concluded that he'd just have to see how the new rule played out. He apologized to today's Sunshine Girl for the interruption in their conversation and continued telling her about a new Bruce Willis action flick.

The following day, he put up a fresh photo. He was just teaching the girl—Dana was her name—how to stand on a windsurfing board when Archie appeared. Looking over Sandy's workplace, he frowned. 'Sorry, Sandy. This has to go. The regulation is clear.'

'Why? Nobody minds. Who's objecting?'

'I don't know. Somebody is. Apparently there have been complaints.'

'Hey, Jenny,' said Sandy. 'Did you complain about my having this picture here?'

'Couldn't care less,' Jenny answered with a smile.

'How many people have complained in your zone?' Sandy asked Archie.

'Well, so far, nobody.'

'And how many people display this kind of picture?'

'About a dozen, I guess. Maybe more,' Archie mumbled.

'So to accommodate zero complaints, you piss off at least a dozen people?'

'It's not me,' Archie protested. 'I already told you. The directive came from above. To improve the atmosphere in the plant, they say, so nobody feels embarrassed or harassed. Maybe the brothers up there know more about complaints than we do. There must have been some. Who's complaining? How am I to know?'

'Okay, then. Tell me, unofficially, in your opinion, who could be bothered by a picture of a young woman in a swimsuit?'

Archie thought about the question. 'Well, maybe someone who's not so young and not so good-looking, who's self-conscious in a swimsuit. Maybe someone who's not a Blue Jays fan—you have to admit, those Blue Jays T-shirts show up a lot. Maybe some fellow past his prime doesn't like being exposed to the charms of youth. Who knows?'

'Look, Archie, this is a respected daily newspaper, read by half a million people, and I'm not going to let anybody decide for me whether I will read it vertically or horizontally.'

The next day, just as Sandy was trying to talk the Sunshine Girl into going dancing that evening, Archie returned with a senior member of the plant's Union leadership.

'Look here, brother,' said the senior rep. 'There have been complaints, enough of them to make the Union and the Company reach a deal and set a new regulation. You'll have to be a good boy and comply by taking down that picture.'

'*You* look, brother,' Sandy retorted. 'Before I comply, I'd like to see the minutes of the meeting that decided the issue. I want to see the discussion and the reasoning behind this ban. Also, I'd love to know who complained. Could you get those minutes for me?'

'What do you need those for? The leadership has decided, after much deliberation. You should trust that they decided correctly.'

'And where is the democratic decision-making, hey?' Sandy was getting into high gear. 'No discussion. Nobody asked us. This was all cooked up without any input from the membership. The white-shirts decided up there, on high, and we're the ones to suffer the consequences.'

Now the senior rep started to raise his voice. 'Democracy depends on the election of the leaders to enact various measures on behalf of the membership. The membership approves important stuff, like the collective agreement, but needn't trouble itself to be involved in every triviality.'

'Triviality! A triviality for those chaps in the Toronto office may be a real big deal for someone on the line, brother. Get those minutes for me, will you, and then I'll decide what to do.'

'Fine, I'll try,' the senior rep said, to defuse the conflict. But when Archie continued his rounds the rep returned to the Union offices where he convened an urgent meeting.

For two days, there were no developments. Sandy was able to work and hold his imaginary conversations without any interference. Once in awhile, mind you, he found his Sunshine Girl agreeing with him about all the Mrs Grundys in the organization.

On the morning of the third day, Archie came by to inform Sandy, quietly, that if his defiance continued, the Union would be obliged to recommend punishment—a day's suspension. Sandy looked at Archie in disbelief, and burst into laughter, though the hilarity was not quite genuine. 'What a beauty, brother,' he said, with heavy irony. 'The Union was established to *protect* the worker from the Company, and now the Union is asking the Company to *suspend* me? Only the Company, not the Union, can suspend. Wonderful. Let me shake your hand, brother, to salute a truly amazing achievement. The whole philosophy of the Union has been turned upside down because of a few silly pictures. Have you brought me those minutes?'

'They say the meeting was not public. The minutes are for participants only.'

'Silly of me to expect anything else. Well, brother, until somebody gives me a valid, common-sense reason for the ban, and a precise explanation of what was agreed upon, and why, we have nothing further to talk about.'

Archie made his rounds, but his heart wasn't in his duties. Personally, he had nothing against displaying the pictures. He had worked on the line once, and back then, he, too, had displayed pictures, some of them rather daring. He was a good Union rep—experienced, well trained, equipped with a healthy spirit of resistance to the rule of supervisors and the general foreman on the floor. He had always fought for his people on the line and kept the Company on the defensive. But suddenly, the conflict wasn't between Union and Company, but between Union and member. In this case, the Company and the Union seemed to be, perish the thought, allies. Archie's world was wobbling. He trusted the Union, both in the plant and nationally. A united stance was necessary. But those arguing loyalties made him irritable. What was he to do?

The following day, he felt a surge of relief. Sandy hadn't displayed his Sunshine Girl. But his relief was short-lived. On her side of the line, Jenny had posted a picture. Archie had no choice but to order its immediate removal. Jenny refused, claiming that it was a photo of her cousin; she was displaying a family portrait. Archie thought she was bluffing, but didn't press the issue and continued his rounds.

The next day, he found that Jenny had posted another picture.

Jenny argued that she could display as many photos of women as she wanted. 'After all,' she said, 'I *am* a woman. I'm not offending myself.'

Archie had no answer to that. The regulation banning photos was vague, except the stipulation that they couldn't be displayed vertically. It was otherwise short on specifics that might guide Archie's judgment and argumentation. Was the main criterion the sex of the subject? Clothing, or the lack of it? Were there different rules for men and women? Was erotic content the dividing line? He asked his superiors, who clarified that the ban was general and covered everybody and everything that might offend anybody. The main criterion was potential to offend. Offensiveness was not defined. Archie's blood pressure began to rise. That evening he discovered his first grey hair. He had trouble sleeping. The whole affair had left cracks in his faith. More than a few times it entered his mind to wonder what the better world that the Union, and he himself, were fighting for would be worth if there was no room in it for pictures of pretty girls in bikinis, and for daydreaming on the assembly line.

Sandy was not dumb. His regular reading of the *Toronto Sun* gave him a decent awareness of what was going on in society. He suspected who his opponents were, and knew what he was up against. He'd be able to keep his Sunshine Girls only if he quit Ford, but if he didn't work at Ford, he wouldn't need them. Well, he wasn't going to give up without a fight. Since he was no longer allowed to converse with his Sunshine Girls, he entertained himself by considering which tactics to employ. He decided that if nobody was willing to tell him the limits of the ban, he would have to test them himself. The military called it reconnaissance through combat. Sandy concluded that launching a few such armed probes might at least be amusing.

A few days later, he enlivened his workplace with a colourful portrait he had found in a book from the public library, which he had copied and enlarged.

Archie's first thought after seeing the portrait was that he wouldn't mind a little flirt with her, but his sense of duty made him frown at the picture and, with some hesitation, say, 'That woman has got to come down!'

'I am beautifying my workstation, Archie. For myself and for others,' Sandy said sweetly. 'This lady is no dime-a-dozen Sunshine Girl. She is art with a capital *A*. Straight from the Pushkin Museum of Western Art in Moscow. Some actress or other. Mr Renoir painted her. You can verify that. The painting is called *Jeanne Samary in a Low-Necked Dress*. You won't seriously claim that the Union stands against art in the workplace, will you? You don't mean to tell me you're offended by the work of a top-flight artist like Mr Renoir. If so, I'd have to consider you a barbarian.'

Throughout the shift, several Union reps came to view the portrait. They scurried away to their offices, where they held a two-day meeting behind closed doors. Perhaps they consulted the national leadership. In the end, they decreed that since the woman in the portrait was of the female sex, and the painting was displayed in a vertical position, the whole exhibit violated the spirit of the regulation and had to be removed immediately.

Five days later, Sandy sent a long letter to the Union in the plant, the National Union, and several major art galleries across the country. In it, he charged that the Canadian Auto Workers Union had initiated a campaign to change the way paintings in galleries could be displayed. All paintings depicting girls, maidens, goddesses, women, nymphs, ladies, matrons, dames, spinsters— females in any shape and form, regardless of their state of dress or undress—would have to be removed from the walls, and laid flat on the floor. Suspended walkways were to be built above them to allow visitors to view and admire them. In the closing paragraph, with the deepest regret, he also anticipated the removal of all portraits of her majesty the Queen from public offices. His main contention was that laws and regulations must treat all members of society equally. He considered the present state of affairs to be particularly discriminatory against workers in the auto industry. The galleries never responded to his letter and the Union sent word that he should stop being silly.

Two weeks later, Sandy found a photo in the library that would blast Archie's mind to smithereens. He made an enlarged Xerox copy and pinned the picture above his workstation. He could hardly wait for Archie's arrival.

As usual, Archie came along shortly before noon. He looked at the picture. His jaw dropped and remained open. From the Sunshine Girls in their bikinis, Sandy had progressed to displaying a girl, or rather a woman, unabashedly showing her bare breasts in public. She was climbing some sort of a barricade, waving a French flag, surrounded by a bunch of armed people. Archie had a vague feeling of recognition, as if he'd seen the painting somewhere before. It had to do with a revolution. The woman was a symbol, and the symbol was positive.

Sandy gestured to the painting. 'Let me introduce you,' he said. 'This lady is *Liberty Leading the People*, just as Mr Delacroix painted her.'

'And why is she leading them half naked?' Archie stammered.

'I guess that's how they used to fight revolutions in Paris,' Sandy offered. 'Maybe the liberation of women was on the agenda, even back then.'

Archie's eyes darted nervously between Sandy and *Liberty*. Words failed him. He turned abruptly on his heel, growled, 'I'll be back,' and walked away glancing over his shoulder as if that revolutionary crowd targeted him.

Sandy winked at Jenny, who gave him a thumbs-up.

The whole Union leadership accompanied Archie when he returned. They formed a semicircle around the painting, and animated discussion ensued. Sandy had to remind them that he had a job to do. 'Either shut down the line,' he said, 'or get out of the way.' As the job took him up and down the line, Sandy caught only snippets of their opinions: *She represents the revolutionary tradition.... She's on our side of the barricade.... But she's topless.... Sure, we approve of what she stands for, but we can't condone.... She's got very nice boobs.... She's not interfering with safety.... Sandy must be pulling our leg....*

Then a booming voice surmounted the clamour. Sandy heard every word with clarity. 'We have a problem, brothers,' a wise man intoned. 'If this scene were to happen today, let's say in Toronto, that woman could certainly be arrested for fomenting revolution, for obstructing the flow of traffic, or maybe for leading an unauthorized gathering of people. But not for exposing her breasts.'

Silence fell. Could this be a loophole? Clearly, this case would have to be brought to the very highest levels of authority. The Union guys shot a few Polaroid photos as documentation. They told Sandy that he was a provocateur, and that they would open a case against him. They made to take down the painting.

At that very moment, a blast of very loud, very sad music sounded from a portable music player on Jenny's worktable, some sort of funeral march—Chopin, maybe Beethoven. *Pam pam pa da dam....*

'What's this?' the Union vice-president exploded.

'Oh, nothing,' Sandy said, innocently. 'We're just disappointed that our Union is the one that's removing Liberty from the workplace, so we wanted to give her an appropriate accompaniment on her farewell journey'.

The Union guys understood that Sandy's trap had just sprung. They hastily vacated the area without a word, with Liberty rolled up and carried off as exhibit A.

The higher-ups deliberated for a long time, and the decision was predictable: Sandy was not allowed to display *Liberty Leading the People.* They recommended magnanimity and tolerance in the disciplinary proceedings against Sandy. The ruling stated that he was pursuing a serious issue, and that exercising some leeway would be preferable to punishment, since they acknowledged some people might be slower than others in comprehending and accepting ongoing societal changes. Besides, Sandy was a good worker—he had no unauthorized absences, he finished his cars, he didn't drink on the job. So he escaped with nothing more than an oral dressing-down and a substantial lecture about the difference between horizontal and vertical.

The tug-of-war over the Sunshine Girl persisted more than six weeks. Spring was past. Yesterday had been the first day of the year Sandy had been able to enjoy the rectangle of sunshine on the floor. The brilliant ray of light appeared for a brief time, somewhat shyly, but long enough to give Sandy an inspiration. It occurred to him that he might be able to project an image of the Sunshine Girl on the wall. He would obey the regulation to a T—the picture itself would be one hundred percent horizontal at all times—but there was no prohibition against projecting an immaterial image vertically, was there? Such a trick might cause an amusing confrontation. But he shelved the idea; he'd toyed with the Union long enough. He wanted no permanent conflict with them. In the long run, he was on their side, and they were on his.

The rectangle of sunshine rectangle returned, day after day. One day, as he watched the slanted shaft of sunlight moving across the concrete floor, Sandy experienced a further flash of illumination. Yes! He'd finally hit on the right approach, the permanent solution that would allow him to keep his Sunshine Girls for good. By offering the Union a loophole, an out, he would meet them halfway. It was such a simple idea, a wonderful idea. He spent three days on the line thinking it over, and concluded that it was faultless.

Sandy spent a whole weekend making calculations, drafting,

measuring, sawing, drilling, planing, screwing, painting, and finally savouring the finished product. On Monday morning, he brought to work the fruit of his labour. He drank his coffee, and, with a minor reorganization of the containers on his worktable, he cleared enough room to place a wedge-shaped lectern, of the sort a musician might use to display his or her score. On it, he lovingly placed a cutout of the day's Sunshine Girl.

Sandy anticipated Archie's visit with great excitement. He wasn't quite sure that the Union rep would come—lately he'd had a tendency to look the other way, or to speed up as he passed Sandy's workstation. But Archie didn't lack the courage to face unpleasant situations, and he refused to shirk his duties, no matter how apprehensive he might be about what Sandy's next trap might be.

Eventually, Archie did arrive. He examined the object on Sandy's workstation and sighed. 'Not another one! How many times do we have to go through this?' His eyes met Sandy's with desperation. 'The girl must be horizontal. She has to be lying on her back. Is this one lying on her back? No, she is not.'

'Ah, but she is!' Sandy claimed. 'It's math, Archie. Horizontal and vertical meet in a right angle—ninety degrees. Correct?'

'Well sure, that's what they told us in school,' Archie agreed grudgingly, not knowing where Sandy was going with this.'

'And one half of ninety is forty-five. Still correct?'

'Yes, that's right.'

'So, we have a basis for dividing the horizontal from the vertical. Whatever's over forty-five degrees is vertical, and so whatever's below forty-five degrees must be horizontal. Now, pay attention. This lectern has an incline of forty-four degrees exactly. That means this beauty is displayed closer to the horizontal axis than the vertical. The girl is resting on her back, according to the wishes of the Union. She meets the regulations.'

'Forty-four degrees?' Archie blurted. 'Are you off your rocker?' Archie appeared aghast, at least at first. But then he calmed down as some of his reasoning returned and Sandy's numbers slowly began to make sense. 'It is smart,' he said, 'but I'm going to have to confiscate the contraption anyway.' He grabbed the lectern and prepared to leave.

'You can measure it as many times as you wish. On the back, you will find the logic in writing, just in case you forget how I explained it to you. Take your time, study it, send it to the experts in Toronto or wherever. I can wait.'

As it turned out, Sandy did wait, almost two weeks. He was on lunch break, eating his sandwich. With his back to the line, facing the aisle, he watched Archie approach, lectern in hand. Sandy smiled as Archie reached the table, placed the lectern on it, and sat down facing Sandy.

'Here you go. Have it back. We measured everything. By the way, the precise angle is forty-three point eight degrees.' He took a deep breath and delivered what sounded like a pre-approved speech. 'We considered your argument about the dividing line, deliberated, consulted the national leadership, and came to the following conclusion: for the sake of a compromise, the Union and the plant leadership have decided to permit your use of the lectern on the grounds that, since it has an incline of less than forty-five degrees, it permits your girl to be displayed lying down, rather than standing up. For the sake of the above-mentioned compromise, and without undue nitpicking, the lectern therefore meets the requirement of horizontality.' Archie sighed, clearly relieved that he hadn't screwed up the official pronouncement. 'So, you've won,' he added, 'and, praise the Lord, so have we.' Archie lit a cigarette and blew out the smoke with satisfaction. 'Otherwise,' he went on, 'your crackpot ideas would turn my hair completely grey.'

Sandy smiled to indicate his readiness to restore peaceful relations, but then a spark of mischief lit his eyes. 'Just lean all the way over to the right, Archie, so you're able to see past that cardboard box. Take a look at the line.'

On the floor, reclining on a piece of cardboard and resting on her elbows in the rectangle of intense sunshine, was Jenny. Her crumpled T-shirt lay next to her. She was smiling, her eyes closed, looking serene, happy even, as she offered her face to the sun's rays … and also her bare breasts.

Archie had a good, long look.

'Well? What about that?' asked Sandy.

Archie cleared his throat and said, with a touch of melancholy, 'There's nothing we can do, brother, and nothing we'd want to do. She's completely within her rights.'

LUCY AND LEO

'Balzac!' Leo shouted, 'She's right out of Balzac!' Nobody on the line paid any attention, much less reacted to the shout, even though there was an edge of horror in Leo's voice. He staggered a bit when he realized what he had just shouted, and how precisely and powerfully it expressed his nebulous but turbulent feelings. He was so flabbergasted by the intensity and immediacy of this insight, well, epiphany, that for a moment he froze like a pillar of salt. He stepped back only when the frame of a car brushed against his midriff and threatened to topple him. He quickly remembered that he was at work, grabbed his gun, and, with a few swift moves, screwed the brake line to the frame.

It wasn't Balzac's name that staggered him. He was familiar with it, having been an avid reader for some seventeen years. His passion for reading had originated at the age of twelve when his aunt gave him a copy of *The Three Musketeers* for his birthday. He'd been charmed by Dumas's storytelling and found himself lured into the landscapes of fictitious worlds and the lives of people he would never meet in real life. He grew to love browsing the extensive offerings of the local public library. In his teenage years, he preferred novels of adventure and exploration. But as he grew older his tastes had matured, and after reading *Literary Lapses* by Stephen Leacock, he extended his interests to other authors. He encountered Balzac's many works several times as he devoured book after book.

Luckily, all the books he'd read came back to serve him again when he started working on the line at Ford. He was bored to death until he discovered that he could bring to mind all those books and even relive some of them. He might try to recall the names of all four servants in *The Three Musketeers*, or the name of the lady in Jack London's *Sea Wolf*. A merry bunch of characters, both heroic good guys and dastardly villains, kept him in pleasant company on the line. Now, it seemed as if one of his literary companions had whispered to him, pitched him a thought that he could recognize and voice. 'That woman *is* a character out of Balzac,' said Leo to himself, now in a low voice and much more calmly.

That woman was Lucy. Treacherous Lucy. For over six years she'd been his partner, sharing his apartment, his table, his bed, and his bank account. They were not married, but neither cared about that. They were happy together without wedding rings and stamped documents. Leo had worked the whole of these past six years at Ford, almost literally, almost slavishly, and moreover gladly, for her. 'Idiot,' he thought bitterly, as he recalled their first meeting.

One morning, after a year working in the Ford body shop, Leo had found himself standing in the cafeteria line in front of a very pretty girl. He paid for her coffee as well as for his own, just to see the surprise on her face when the cashier told her that her coffee was taken care of. She thanked him for the unexpectedly bright beginning to her morning. They sat together, and she started to talk. She was a student, hired for the summer to work on line two. She hoped to make enough money to pay for university courses in the fall. Four months on the line should bring in at least ten grand—enough to tide her over the first two semesters. The year before, she'd attended classes at the local community college, studying to become a social worker, but she'd developed higher goals. Her new ambition was to study anthropology at university. University was the ticket to a happy life, she said. They began meeting in the cafeteria more and more often, and then they got together outside of work as well. Before summer yellowed into fall, they were in love. Lucy's job at

Ford ended, and it was only logical to share an apartment. It was cheaper for them both.

Lucy drove daily to the university, and Leo to the Ford plant. Within the limits imposed by her schoolwork, she took good care of him. She made the beds in the morning, prepared sandwiches, and packed Leo's lunch box. Now and then she cooked a full meal, especially over the weekends. She tidied the apartment, did the washing, cleaned the bathroom. That spring she successfully completed her first year of university courses, and both faced the question of whether it made sense for her to return to Ford to work on the line again. Last year's funds had been completely spent, though both had lived frugally. So one Saturday evening they sat down at the kitchen table to discuss the issue.

Lucy had presented a proposal, a long-term plan. She must have given it a lot of thought, because it was well prepared and detailed. She should be studying full time now, she said, including in the summer. Progressing through her courses should be her number one priority, so as to complete the program as soon as humanly possible. It was doable, she thought, if Leo agreed to support her, just temporarily. Once she had her degree, she assured him it would be a piece of cake to land a job earning at least three times what he was making. Then she would be the breadwinner and support him if he wanted to take courses. Or else he could stay home, maybe start a small business. Alternatively—and this, she affirmed, was the better idea—both would work while they saved and invested at least one full salary. If they continued to live modestly, within fifteen years, twenty at the most, they'd have a million dollars in the bank and both would be able to retire and live life to the fullest, to have their own house, a luxury car, and to travel around the world without any financial worries, because they would be rich and secure. And happy. Just imagine, retirement before fifty! No more waking up before six in the morning. Eventually no more line, no more sore back, no more Ford. A permanent holiday, day after day, year after year. He could see the beauty of her vision, couldn't he? He trusted her calculations, didn't he? She was a university student, so she knew what she was talking about.

Leo had felt he had no choice but to agree. He succumbed not only to Lucy's eloquence, but also to his respect for the intelligent and the educated. He didn't know where this deference came from—perhaps it had infiltrated his mind through his reading. He deeply admired the authors, those demigods who created whole worlds that he loved to visit, and that enriched his life immensely. Those writers had to be educated and intelligent to come up with such unique characters and compelling stories. Leo was anything but dim, but formal education had never attracted him. In school his natural inquisitiveness always led him to read outside the curriculum—and into his teachers' bad books. He'd always felt more restricted by what he was supposed to be learning than enriched, and he had heaved a big sigh of relief when the doors of his high school closed behind him for good. But having an educated girlfriend stroked his ego, so she went back to her books and he returned to the line.

Lucy studied for hours and hours and hours. It looked like hard work—harder than working on the line was for Leo. Sometimes she barely managed to squeak by with a passing grade on an exam. Twice she failed, despite her best efforts. She didn't share her difficulties with Leo, didn't want to spoil his image of her, the one she'd been carefully cultivating. She never failed to remind him that higher education wasn't for everyone, that not everybody possessed the unique combination of intelligence and tenacity or, as she liked to put it, the requisite grey matter and glutei maximi required to succeed in such a rarefied environment. Occasionally, she had to pooh-pooh Leo's common sense and original ways of thinking, by pointing out that 'Professor Mulligan's opinion is …' or 'Professor Carter believes that …' Leo didn't dare argue with anybody who was a professor.

Step by step, Lucy had managed to climb up onto the pedestal she had been building for herself. Little by little she became a sort of idol for Leo, one that he could admire, worship, serve. Each completed semester added additional height to that pedestal. She had transformed herself into his queen, his goddess, though she occasionally had trouble recalling which goddess was in charge of intelligence. For her, he had trudged in to Ford, working the line day after day, and bringing her sacrifices in the form of weekly paycheques. Tiny niggles aside, he hadn't minded. He'd been in love and happy, and though he lived a relatively deprived life, it was all for the promise of a richer, fuller life in the future. When Lucy completed her bachelor's degree (by the skin of her teeth) she and Leo had thrown a big party. Everybody congratulated not only her, but Leo as well. He was elated, proud of her, and proud of himself for having such a smart and educated partner.

It hadn't taken long for Lucy to suggest that she should continue her education with a master's degree. Leo had been taken aback at first, but he soon agreed. He liked the prospect of having a partner, possibly a wife, with a master's degree, not to mention the fact that she would be making much more money than she could with a mere B.A. Graduate study might be a bit more expensive, but he reasoned that she'd bring in a little money as a teaching assistant. Two more years, two and a half, tops. Eventually, all their sacrifices would pay off.

That summer, as a reward, they'd treated themselves to a week-long vacation at a campground on Lake Erie. When they weren't at the beach, Lucy immersed herself in her demanding scholarly texts while Leo indulged in his entertaining literary books.

The following two and a half years were really trying. Lucy had clearly hit the limit of her grey matter. She studied so hard Leo sometimes thought her brain-cells were giving off puffs of smoke, and her ass was getting flatter than two pancakes, but even so, she had to take a couple of courses twice. It made the studying more expensive. She also bought several ergonomic office chairs, one after another, seeking relief for her sore butt.

At about the same time Leo's car had given up the ghost and had to be consigned to a junkyard. He needed a car to get to work, and even a second-hand Taurus set him back five thousand bucks. To cover the installments, he had taken on two hours of extra overtime during the night shift. That involved working at the exit water test, checking to make sure the finished cars were watertight. As jobs at Ford went, it wasn't so tough. He just had to squat a lot. But it was still a burden after working the ten hours of his regular shift. He was bone tired. Lucy studied, studied, studied, and Leo worked, worked, worked, worked. He had no energy to concentrate, so he gave up on reading. Once home from work, he fell into bed and slept almost until his next shift.

Finally, Lucy dragged herself through her thesis, and graduation came. During the ceremony and the following festivities, Leo had had to fight off his sleepiness. But the cheering and the celebrations signified impending relief. Now Lucy would start making money, and he could go back to his regular ten-hour shifts and his books. They were finally about to enter the second phase of their plan to become millionaires and retire before fifty. Hallelujah!

The week after Lucy's graduation, Leo had worked the night shift, and because he had forgotten to cancel the extra overtime, he'd been automatically booked for it. He'd had to cover the water test job for another week. When he returned home, just before seven on Tuesday morning, Lucy's car was not in the parking lot. She wasn't at home, either. He was too tired to care. He shrugged his shoulders, drank a beer, and collapsed into bed. She still hadn't come home late in the afternoon when the alarm clock jerked him out of sleep. A short while later he found a letter on her pillow.

Lucy wrote that she was leaving him and moving to Toronto, a city that could offer her much more room to pursue her career. He hadn't had much time for her lately. He'd been neglecting her. But the main thing was that she now belonged in the elite group of people decorated with not just one degree, but two, and her education really obliged her to seek out new friends and a life partner whose achievements were commensurate with her new status and elevated spiritual needs. Farewell, she wrote. Life with you was okay, but my future lies elsewhere, and with someone else.

At least, that was the gist.

Leo had collapsed to his knees as if somebody had smacked his head with a two-by-four. He curled up on his side, his knees drawn up to his chest. He was struck dumb. But eventually, habit took over. Habit dressed him, pushed him out the door and into the Taurus, drove him to the plant, led him to the line, worked for him. When he returned home in the morning, there was nothing to do but fall into bed and lose consciousness.

The next night on the line, he concluded that his life was worthless. Lucy's words had destroyed his whole world, blasted his universe to smithereens. He found it impossible to believe that his betrayed and broken heart could possibly keep on beating. His tortured and keening soul hurt so much that even death could add nothing to the pain. The best escape from this hell would be to buy a piece of rubber hose, drive somewhere out in the woods, stick one end of the hose over the exhaust and the other end into the car. In a short while the pain would be all over. *She* would be over, as would the exhaustion, the treachery, the humiliation.

When he drove home in the morning, it was too early to buy the hose. In the afternoon, he was still too tired to kill himself. In his present state, who knew, he might screw up even his suicide. And missing a shift wasn't his habit. He postponed the suicide until the weekend. He slept through the whole of Saturday. That evening, he had two beers, ate something, had two more beers, and went back to sleep. Around noon on Sunday, he woke up somewhat refreshed. His head was clearer. To his amazement, he discovered that his shattered heart was still pumping blood. The sun still shone, the birds still sang. At the same time, as far as he knew, no lightning had struck the bitch for her treachery. The earth had not opened up to swallow her. Her knife in his back hurt like hell, but perhaps it hadn't been lethal.

After ten more days of such miserable thrashing, while tornadoes of memory scattered his mental furniture, the chaos of his mind, the hatred, had begun to coalesce around the idea of revenge. He couldn't accept leaving his humiliation unanswered. He had to deliver a counterpunch a hundred times more devastating than the one she'd landed. He had to wreak a tremendous revenge in the great style of the Count of Monte Cristo. He had to destroy her utterly, annihilate her, erase every trace of her, or else his soul would not find peace. He had plenty of time to spin his devilish plans while he worked on the line. He would find out who she was living with, where she was employed, and which bank took care of her accounts. Then he'd work to undercut all three pillars of her life, one after another. Her life would collapse and she'd be buried in the rubble of her dreams. Yes! And in the end, there he'd be, standing to one side with arms folded, wrapped in his cloak like the Count of Monte Cristo, watching the smoking ruins of her life and enjoying the sweet music of her wailing. Ha! It was entertaining, even therapeutic, to daydream in this way. A few days of imagining such agreeable comeuppance managed to calm his rage, but then reason crept in, dispelling the emotional heat from his mind. He had begun to realize that, once again, he had allowed his thoughts to orbit around her. He had thought of nothing but her. Her! Again her! Forcing her way back into the centre of his life. No way, he had said to himself. He'd wasted enough time on her. How many years, how much money and energy had the Count of Monte Cristo sacrificed to his mollify his soul? If, as an old man, he'd ever looked back at his whole life, would he still believe the revenge was worth it?

Standing with one foot on the frame line and the other in

bookland, Leo had been visited with the epiphany that made him shout, out of the blue, 'She's right out of Balzac!'

Leo's triumphant shout marked the moment when he rebounded from the rock bottom. Suddenly, Lucy's duplicity wasn't so absurd, so inexplicable. The pages of Balzac were teeming with single-minded people who pursued their goals regardless of the number of bodies they have to step on. Leo had always found Balzac's characters to be caricatures, exaggerated out of proportion, not reflective of actual living people so much as products of a pessimistic imagination. It was why Leo didn't count Balzac among his favourite authors. In a flash, he realized that Mr Balzac hadn't been imagining but rather observing, then inviting into his novels living people from the sidewalks, shops, and salons of Paris. Such one-dimensional people *did* exist in reality. His Lucy, his sweet little angel, his idol, his queen on her pedestal, was one of them. He himself would cut a good figure as a character in Balzac—naive, love-blinded, stupidity incarnate. Good God, he'd been a colossal idiot.

Yes. Colossal. He had to face the truth. An idiot. Why? He had an ocean of time on the line, and certain questions kept drifting back to him, as if towed in by the tides. Why hadn't he noticed from the very beginning that Lucy was nothing but a cynical gold-digger? How could he have been blind to the fact for six long years? He guessed because nobody expected a gold-digger to set her snare on the line at Ford. The gold-digger's hunting grounds were among the big mansions, yachts, Rolls-Royces, Ferraris, and fine art auctions. Journalists were always saying that the working class was exploited and underpaid and ought to be offered better wages, but probably Lucy hadn't been reading those newspapers or magazines that published such journalists. Leo admitted he'd been naive, a simpleton, an innocent with an open heart. She had outsmarted him. After all, she had the B.A. and the M.A. She made the plans. She set the terms. She was the intelligent one.

'A whore! She's a whore!' Leo shouted now. Again, nobody reacted. Yelling on the line, snippets of singing, bursts of profanity, a hammer banging on a metallic railing, shouts of 'Yes, baby,' generated by some rock riff heard through headphones, choral chanting of 'Heads are gonna roll' whenever a supervisor chewed somebody out—all that made up the usual aural background of the line. Nobody who'd spent time in a factory would be surprised. A whore! And even that wasn't a strong enough word! Whores were selling just their bodies while this monster, Lucy, sold her whole self and then some. Thoughts, morals, emotions, dignity, conscience, character, integrity, future … all of herself for sale … and him, Leo, too. Leo's mind was a raging volcano. But this outburst proved to be *the* turning point, the real catharsis for Leo. The word 'whore', so passionately spat out of his mouth, landed with full force on his mental image of Lucy on her pedestal. It smashed the head and toppled the body. He watched it fall in slow motion. It fell, fell, all the way to the ground where it shattered into fifty pieces. Leo's eyes were flashing as he kept on shouting variations on whore! Hooker! Harlot! Strumpet! Hustler! Tramp! Bimbo! Slut! Tart! And, once more, whore! Each shouted word filled him with a strange satisfaction, as if the insults cleared and disinfected his mind, removing all remnants of his admiration for her. Through them he stomped the shards of her image with his safety boots, grinding them into smithereens, into dust, into nothingness.

It was only a few weeks later, assured that Lucy had really lost her power over him, that no idealized image of her controlled his thoughts, that the sacred cow had been reduced to a common one, only then did a wave of cold sweat wash over him. 'Shit,' he shouted, 'that was close!' All of a sudden he realized how many more years he might have lost, vegetating in a state of suspended living, if she had stayed. He might have wasted his whole life waiting for the day they had enough money to start living. Hot and cold flashes ran up and down his spine. He alternately cursed her and—here was another pivot in his thinking—blessed her for running away in the nick of time. She'd stolen no more than six years and some thirty grand—a small price to pay for a life lesson. He might have wasted many more years, decades even, in pursuit of her foolish ambition to buy a million bucks-worth of future happiness. That would have been the real disaster. The thirty grand was nothing—after all, there'd been good days and nights with her, satisfying and frequent sex. Hiring a hooker every weekend would have cost more. Dating other girls would have incurred considerable costs—for dinners, for flowers, for wine. From a monetary point of view, which was Lucy's preferred way of looking at things, he hadn't had that bad a deal.

You either live now or not at all. The lesson was priceless.

Now that he recognized that Lucy was a character out of Balzac, it dawned on him that he didn't have to bother with revenge—the bomb of vengeance was already ticking away inside her. She was a fraud; she would try to swindle her way through life, and the dishonesty would catch up with her in the end. There was a chance that her next partner, some educated slyboots, would see through her and leave her cold. If she stayed single, how long would it take her to amass a million bucks? He suspected that her salary calculations were the result of wishful thinking. Time would stretch out longer and longer, until old age brought about dwindling energy and ill health started visiting her. She would never have enough to start living. In her golden years there she'd be, sitting on the balcony of her tiny apartment, watering her flowers and wondering what might have been if … She had been dishonest her whole life, and so life would be dishonest with her. Was that his own thought or a quotation? Sometimes he was tickled by his own insights.

Five months after Lucy's departure, Leo was pondering her depravities less and less frequently. He didn't want to be pondering them at all, but he still had to spend his days at work. Life on the line kept bringing him new questions, one after another, and offering him plenty of time to contemplate them. Would he ever be able to trust a woman again? Was he to remain a bachelor? Did his favourite musketeer, Athos, think about another marriage after the betrayal of his first wife? At first Leo was confused, because his answers to some of those questions seemed strange. The new answers didn't match his old thinking. His insight questioning the gratification of Count Monte Cristo's revenge, or his discovery that Lucy was carrying her downfall within herself—where did they come from? They didn't fit his image of himself. Eventually, he decided that some sort of new self was trying to displace the old one. He felt as if his old self was being carried away by the line, little by little, old cells carried away with each brake line, obsolete neurons left behind on each frame that he worked on. New thinking was an upgrade. He was becoming more vital, more thoughtful, smarter.

Leo found a new apartment. He didn't want to stay in the old one with her ghost hovering there, didn't want to run the risk that she might one day knock on his door. He bought new furniture, a big La-Z-Boy recliner and a good lamp so he could enjoy reading in comfort. With great satisfaction, he threw out anything connected to her—especially the bed with the springs that were hurting his ribs. He donated all six of her fancy office chairs to Goodwill. They were like new.

He spent his summer vacation in Western Canada, exploring the Rocky Mountains. His travels had no specific goal; he just wanted to escape the ever-present rumble of technology at Ford. He craved the green silence of uncivilization. He browsed, he followed his nose. Sometimes he slept in a tent, sometimes a motel. He ate well and breathed deeply. He was relaxed. At times, in the presence of the granite majesty of the mountain peaks, he was able to stop thinking altogether. The endless forests, the vast blue skies, the flickering of gazillions of stars at night, all of it offered much more fodder for his flights of fancy than the line ever had. He felt like a wilted flower absorbing rain, rejuvenated, as the marvelous, oxygen-rich mountain air breathed new energy into his body. He preferred campgrounds with nothing but an outhouse and a faucet with potable water. He felt better without any people around. He was alone in a different way than he was on the line. He could think, but he didn't have to. Out here, he realized how much this disaster had enriched him. His personal cataclysm had removed the scales from his eyes and cleared his mind. How much more mature he'd become, how much he had expanded in knowledge and understanding. At times, he was tempted to feel that he might be … reasonably intelligent. Where was this idea coming from?

'The books!' he shouted into the quiet. 'It's the books!' As he was the only living soul in this particular wild campground, nobody paid any attention. Years and years of reading had trained his mind just as work on the line had trained his body. Almost two decades of reading had taught him to think a little like the authors he admired, to adopt those ways of seeing the world he found so enchanting. Their lessons had taught him to decipher Lucy, to understand her, to recognize his predicament. Instinctively, he had read his situation like a novel, with Lucy and himself as the characters. Those thousands of pages he had devoured had served as his own university. He'd been a far better student than Lucy, had learned more from books than she had from all her anthropology courses, and his education had been incomparably more entertaining.

It was a very different Leo who marched back onto the line after his vacation. He didn't know what he might do with his new understanding of himself, but he knew that the line would keep bringing him new questions, and that he would have plenty of time to wrestle with them.

He worked for one hour, for three hours, when suddenly he felt a huge surge of energy. It came from something he whispered to himself, so softly that he couldn't even hear the words over the rumbling of the line and all the other ambient noise. To hear himself properly, he now planted his feet firmly, raised his arms in a gesture of victory, and yelled for the whole Ford plant to hear: 'Hey Leo! You're a regular genius!'

Nobody paid any attention.

FROM THE NEW WORLD

The ax has finally fallen, splitting the plant into two halves. Half the workers will go home for good, while just enough will remain to cover one shift.

Ambrose is among those eligible to go home for good. The magic number—the sum of age and years of seniority—has always been eighty-five. That number qualifies a worker for immediate retirement with full pension. But the magic number has now been set at eighty. Ambrose has been working at the plant for close to twenty-five years and is pushing fifty-six years of age. His number is almost eighty-one.

Retirement. What a strange notion. It feels like only yesterday that he started working for Ford, but it's been a quarter century. He has hardly noticed the time pass. Maybe that's because the flow of time here is so monotonous. Work on the line makes one hour much like the next, one day like any other. Twenty-five years … and now, out of the blue, the chance to retire stares him in the face. A pension always seemed like something so distant it was almost mythical. Pensions are for white hairs, and he's still a youngster. Merely saying yes to retirement will throw him in among the old folks overnight.

The news isn't altogether surprising. Rumours have been circulating around the plant for months, but nobody took them seriously. After all, not long ago this plant was considered the most profitable Ford operation in North America. Within the last decade, its workers have won for the Company first the silver and then the gold J.D. Power Award, the prestigious award for best assembled car, domestic or foreign. But the overlords in Detroit have decided to deep-six this plant. The decision buries half now: the remaining half will follow within about three years. Up the line, somebody slowly strikes the railings with a hammer and it sounds to Ambrose like the tolling of funeral bells.

Ambrose's mind feels like it has split in two, just like the plant. If an observer were to get close to Ambrose, close enough to place a stethoscope on his forehead, it would reveal to anyone who cared to listen the terrible rumble of battle raging in his mind. His body has had more than its fill of hard labour over the last twenty-five years, and it's clamouring for immediate departure, for quitting right now, in the middle of this shift. But while Ambrose's body is ready to leave, his mind insists there are serious arguments for staying. So he hesitates. Even a casual observer could see his work sputter, moving in fits and starts. Now and then, it looks like he freezes for a moment. Twice he has forgotten to hit the button that scrolls down the display telling him what kind of battery to install in the car. No wonder his supervisor has stormed in twice to inquire what's going on with him today. If Ambrose, steady, reliable Ambrose, is causing problems, the whole universe must be on the verge of collapse.

Ambrose has known for a while that his health is gradually eroding. It's almost imperceptible, invisible—a tiny bit of his health sacrificed to every car. Ambrose has worked on about three million vehicles. The math says it all. He's getting close to the bottom of the barrel on energy; the battery of his own body is far from fully charged. There are mornings when it barely gets him going. The life expectancy of his joints and sinews is not what it used to be, either. The long-term effects of work on the line are permanent, irreversible. Sooner or later, the full bill will come due.

Just consider the hands—ordinary, calloused human hands. Every job on the line involves the hands in some way, whether it requires you to grab, snatch, squeeze, hold, press, carry, pull, grip, manipulate, or some combination thereof. Or maybe the job calls for working with a gun that vibrates, carrying thirty pounds of metal to the place of installation, resisting the inertia of the heavy mass of some fixture that you have to push or pull, like the batteries Ambrose is now installing on the line. No matter what job you're doing, it can't be done without hands. A hand can stand a whole lot, but its capacity to endure and regenerate is not limitless. Over the years, the fingers get used to holding things. Their natural position becomes curved, and they resist straightening without the aid of hot water and exercise. Imagine standing in front of a bank machine with fingers curled into your palms like talons. They're so stiff you can't even enter your PIN. You have money in the bank, but you can't get at it. The damn fingers won't work. It's a fitting metaphor for the cost of the job. But it's not just the hands that are affected; one could easily move up the arm: wrist, elbow, shoulder, and so on. The whole being, mind and body, is marked by working on the assembly line. So what is it that might keep a worker here?

Ambrose suspects that it's momentum that keeps him and his fellow Fordmates going, momentum and the manacles of habit. The line is the backbone of his life; everything is organized around its requirements. Working on the line isn't so bad, well, except for maybe the first few years on killer jobs. But working here has meant security for his family. It has paid for his house, for his children's education, for the occasional vacation, for reasonably comfortable day-to-day living. Once, money and benefits and security were vital. Today? Not anymore, not really. He has twice what he needs, and he doesn't need all that much. The pension package would not represent a disastrous drop in his income.

Ambrose, like everyone else who worked in the plant, has known for some time that this *Titanic* has been taking on quite a bit of water. Should he stay with her a little longer, or jump ship?

There were times in his life when Ambrose had made quitting a habit. After he'd earned his B.A., he quit his first job after less than half a year because he felt so oppressed by the nine-to-five routine. He stayed a month longer in the next job. After the freedom of childhood and the relative freedom of university, he believed that being tied to a job would prevent him from living his life, so he rebelled. He went through five jobs in three years before fleeing to British Columbia. He took on all kinds of jobs there, from operating the lift at a ski resort to cutting grass on a golf course. In between, he washed dishes in a restaurant, rented skis and ski boots, sold lift tickets in the resort office, and slung drinks as a barman. When his skiing was good enough, he volunteered for ski patrol. His freewheeling years! Full of wonderful company, lots of beer, girls as numerous as snowflakes and willing to melt under a bit of eloquence. He thrived, leaping from job to job, never charming the same girl twice. For four years, he lived and loved the hectic, freewheeling lifestyle. But then the enjoyment started to wane. Though his passion for skiing kept him in the mountains for another season, living hand-to-mouth and out of a suitcase ceased to be so much fun. Escape from routine had become a routine.

The need for some predictability and stability in his life had brought him back home. He'd found a wonderful girl, Susan, and married her. They both wanted children. He'd been lucky to land the job at Ford, though what an ordeal it was at first! In those first months, he wanted so many times to escape. Better to be freezing in a snowstorm at the ski lift, he thought, or weeding sand traps at a golf course for minimum wage. He'd be poor, but he'd be free. He couldn't run away, though, and, oddly enough, he didn't really want to. Children came. Instead of a house in the city, he and Susan bought a nice side-split on an acre-sized plot. They had a mortgage. They had to furnish their home. They had to pay property taxes. What happens to a man in such circumstances at such a point in his life? Somehow, his mind starts playing him like a fiddle. He never cared much about money, but bringing home a decent weekly paycheque became a source of satisfaction, even pride. What had caused the change? The kiss of a beloved wife? The tiny bundle with big eyes that, two years later, learned to call him Daddy? Marital hormones? Paternal hormones? Who can tell.

Then Ambrose first heard the murmurings of cutbacks at the plant. Susan had rejoiced that they would spend more time together. His eldest son, an adult, and on his own, remarked, 'It's high time. Your head is grey enough,' adding that he was referring to what was inside it, not what was on it. Ambrose laughed, but privately felt a little upset. Had his mind really turned grey? But when he scrolled through family photos from the boys' childhood and compared them to more recent images, he had to admit that Pete was right. He used to play soccer with the boys. He'd taught them baseball, built a tree house for them, rode bikes with them, spent whole days with them at the beach. But it wasn't long before the line limited such wasteful expenditures of his energies. It planted small questions in the back of his mind: *Are you willing to ache through the whole shift tomorrow if you go out and teach your boys skiing today? Will your legs last the whole shift after an afternoon playing hockey with them?* Without his realizing it, the line gradually, sneakily, flooded his mind, and, like a tyrant, started to dictate what he wanted and didn't want. It wrestled the reins of his life from his own hands until it had him tamed. Completely. He'd compensated for his waning external life with intense daydreaming about any number of adventures and exertions. Dreaming produced no aches in his body. But he had to ask himself honestly: after so many long years in this plant—was he *living*? He was mortified by the extent of the damage inflicted on his mind. He felt as though he was looking in the mirror for the first time in twenty-five years. *This cannot be me*, he thought.

Time to grab a jacket and go outside for a smoke. Yes, now he has to go outside to enjoy a cigarette. It was one of the small pleasures of the line that had been taken away when anti-smoking legislation came down from Ottawa. It spoiled the whole atmosphere of the plant for the smokers. You like a smoke? Out! In the rain, the freezing wind, the snow. For the first two years after the ban came down from Ottawa, the Company, with the agreement of the Union, looked the other way. Back then, common sense still counted for something. In a space of about five hundred metres by five hundred metres and a height of five storeys, at least ten thousand people would have to be smoking to produce any detectable second-hand smoke. Ford employed only three hundred. But then a few employees began claiming that they were allergic to cigarette smoke. They formed a posse and started a crusade against smokers. Some of the crusaders hadn't previously been allergic to smoke, and some claimed allergies that seemed to be rather selective, manifesting themselves on workdays and only in the plant. Witnesses claimed that on Saturday nights some of those same crusaders were observed spending hours in bars where you couldn't see the far wall through the smoke. For that kind of place, the ban made sense. But detecting the slightest whiff of smoke in the plant, the crusaders followed the trail to the source like bloodhounds and denounced any smoker to the higher-ups. Finally, their efforts, along with relentless pressure from Ottawa, made the Company and the Union deny common sense and give in. At least the exiles now have a covered patio, with a few tables and benches, so they don't have to get soaked.

Wow, what a bluebird day, though it's biting cold. There was freezing rain overnight, and all the branches, the wires, and the fence are encased in crystals of ice. Everything in sight has been turned into a scintillating kingdom of cut crystal. With the icy blue sky above, and the sun still low over the horizon, everything shimmers and sparkles. Silence embraces everything. Ambrose would love to stay out here while the moment is so magical and rare. Silence, peace of mind, beauty, motion arrested. He would love ... it doesn't matter. So long, sunshine, fresh air, natural beauty. His watch tells him it's time to go back into the artificial light of the artificial world of the plant.

Back to the batteries. There are a hundred and thirty of them to finish before the next break. Check the teletype, choose the prescribed battery, pick it up with the pneumatic hoist, swing it under the hood, place it in the battery tray, secure it with a wedge, tighten it with the gun. One of the easier jobs.

Harold brings a new pallet of batteries with his forklift. 'Go outside and check out that glass kingdom,' Ambrose tells him. 'Today is the first time I've even considered saying thank you to that anti-smoking gang; if it wasn't for them I'd have missed out on all that beauty.'

Harold chuckles and when he sees that the line has stopped, comes to share the newest bit of gossip. 'Did you hear, those crusaders landed themselves in a nice little pickle. They caught a fellow in a white shirt and tie who was slowly walking up and down the aisles, now and then stopping and intently following the goings on of the line. He was puffing on a thick cigar, really enjoying it. A cigar! The posse threatened to press charges and send them up the whole chain of command, right up to the highest places. It transpired that the accused had just come down from there, being the plant manager on an inspection tour of his realm. I wonder who's going to win this one.'

Now where was he? Ah, yes. How to free himself from the manacles of habit.

Hesitations aside, Ambrose thinks that escape isn't a bad idea—unexpected and requiring mental adjustment, but not bad. Leaving Ford would mean becoming his own master for the first time in his life. Until now he has always been subordinate to someone else: his parents, his schoolteachers, then all the bosses and supervisors, general foremen and directors he'd had over the years, all the way up to Mr Ford, III—or was it IV? Well, whatever his dynastic number was.

Ambrose used to have more fun here. Everybody did. The small pleasures that used to brighten the days have been sliced away bit by bit. Regulations have multiplied, increasing the tension in the air. Smoke a cigarette inside, where it's warm? Illegal! Display any picture of a girl or a woman? Come on, that kind of brazen action will land you before a tribunal. Get caught pulling the wrong type of prank on a humourless colleague and nobody will bet a dime on your future at Ford. The Union has even established a full-time position just to keep up with all the regulations and monitor compliance with the ever-developing ideological interpretations of interpersonal relations.

A government safety audit added even more regulations. Everybody now has to wear safety shoes and safety glasses, regardless of the job. If you happen to be on quality control for finished cars and the glasses prevent you from seeing a tiny scratch on the paint, tough luck, for you as well as the customer. Driving finished cars off the line to the rolls test? You now have to buckle up. Testing safety belts by holding them in your hand while slamming on the brakes to see if they catch? Same thing. Drivers have to buckle up in every vehicle with a running engine, period. Even forklift guys have to buckle up, though they are required to climb up and down about a hundred and fifty times per shift, to open a box or straighten a tray or collect the cardboard. All that buckling and unbuckling, maybe half an hour per shift spent fiddling with the safety belt, with the additional possibility of disrupting supply to the line. All for a vehicle that never moves fast enough to make safety belts necessary. Just to satisfy the bureaucrats. The Chronomeister must be beside himself, seeing the efforts of a lifetime fizzle like foam on his beer.

No, the future of this plant doesn't look rosy. In a few years, all these regulatory decrees will either push the price of our Fords into Rolls-Royce or Lamborghini territory, or they'll choke the plant completely. With so many regulations in effect, some will inevitably contradict others, and it will become impossible to start the line at all without violating some rule.

Much has changed since Ambrose started at Ford. Most of it is not for the better.

Three days after the spectacle of freezing rain, the plant shuts down mid-afternoon. Everybody goes home. The forecast calls for a major snowfall, maybe even a blizzard. The following morning, the radio announces that the Ford plant has cancelled the morning shift because the supply of parts is delayed. Ambrose goes back to bed. He enjoys a late breakfast at about ten o'clock, and with the storm over, he decides to give himself a rare treat: a day of skiing. He has long neglected his passion, but on this day he will go skiing, not in addition to working on the line but instead of it. His legs shouldn't be any the worse for the neglect.

The local ski hill is full of colourfully dressed people in bubbly moods. After the storm, the snow is just as good as in the Rockies, and Ambrose hums a tune while he skis along. Skiing calls for living in the moment. It pushes every mundane concern out of a skier's mind, temporarily erases all worries. Ambrose skies all the runs, again and again. He hasn't enjoyed skiing so much in a long time. He feels joyful, worry-free. He shares a lift ride with a white-haired man in a red jacket, who asks him, point-blank, if he'd like to become a ski instructor. 'You have the abandon of a true skier. I would hire you right away.' After disembarking at the top, the man disappears as if he has turned himself into a snowflake. *Perhaps he's a fairy godfather*, Ambrose thinks.

The possibility of spending winters on those slopes, doing what he loves, delights Ambrose. Unable to get his fill, he skis until late into the afternoon.

Finally, he takes a break. He sits on a bench in front of the chalet, sipping his coffee.

Suddenly, his retirement dilemma distills itself into a question as straightforward and inexorable as a mathematical formula: Do you want to keep working for Mr Ford? *No, I don't.* Do you have to keep working for Mr Ford? *No, I don't.* All right, then. *It's a done deal, Mr Ford, here's my hand on it.*

The following morning, first thing, Ambrose drops into the Union office to ask them to place his name on the retiree list. He heads towards his workstation on the line, his steps light. He feels transformed, as if by a flick of a magic wand, perhaps belonging to that fairy godfather he met on the slopes. Ambrose dances through his shift, smiling like a renaissance cherub. He feels like singing. The battle behind his forehead has died down. The countdown can begin. His retirement date has been set for May 1, so that's about ninety, no, exactly eighty-seven days. Those days will be a lot easier to get through than the similar probation period he endured at the start of his work on the line.

Now that he has joined the community of those leaving, he finds that a few shared his hesitations. Some greet each other by declaring the number of days remaining before their retirement. Some cross off the days with bold red *x*'s on a calendar, while others do so only in their minds. One creative guy has spent quite a few days turning a tailor's tape measure into a unique countdown tool. He says he picked up the custom during compulsory military service in his country. Each centimetre sports a different colour, and the dividing lines are perforated. He displays the multicoloured tape at his workstation and ceremonially snips off one centimetre at the end of every shift, so he always knows exactly how many more days he has to go. Why the tape measure? Maybe he just missed the day in school when subtraction was covered. Maybe seeing is believing.

For Ambrose, this countdown takes on the timeworn image of the light at the end of the tunnel. His decision has transported him from the inky depths of the tunnel to a place within sight of the light-filled exit. He looks out on a white slope full of colourfully dressed people. He sees the lift, the blue sky above. He knows that his journey into the light will last no more than seventy days, then just sixty. It is as if he is walking on railway ties, one tie for each step, one step per day. Fifty more.... Forty more.... Finally he'll emerge from the tunnel for good, able to turn to his right or his left or up—up that lift!—anywhere, so long as he's off those parallel rails that remind him so much of the line.

Happy, muted prattling enters his mind, and, with it, quiet music of the classical kind.

Two distinct groups of people now join Ambrose on the smokers' patio. Those remaining discuss the good jobs that will be available to them, while soon-to-be retirees ponder their anticipated hours of leisure. Golf all day. Skiing on the local hill. Travel and photography. Reading all the books they've bought, including the ones they never have time to finish because they have to make it to this stupid line on time. Many plan to revive the dreams of their younger, pre-Ford days, dreams that the line almost erased, aborted, carried away. One woman studied to be a concert pianist, but had to abandon the piano because work on the line reduced the agility of her fingers. Now she's looking forward to training her fingers again, if only to perform for herself. Another fellow once loved playing with words and even wrote poetry as a teenager. He has dreamed for years about becoming a writer—maybe it's his time. Others that Ambrose has known for years as figures in blue coveralls now reveal the various talents they've allowed to fall fallow, talents they plan to revisit, to give a fresh chance to spring up and flourish. This one wants to build a kiln and try his hand at pottery. This one has a green thumb and hopes to open her own gardening business. Another is a virtuoso with dough. She is thinking of opening a bakery. This fellow will be able to spend hours and hours restoring vintage cars in his garage. Another intends to restore antique furniture. Youthful dreams have a remarkable resilience.

Ambrose intends to accept the offer of the fairy godfather and become a ski instructor. He'll golf in the summers. If it proves to be too expensive, he'll offer to cut the club's fairways in exchange for green fees. He's sure he still remembers how to do it.

Last fortnight … Last week … His mind spends less and less time on the line. It's soaring about, reveling in impending freedom from all those regulations. Bye-bye, safety shoes. Farewell, coveralls. Adieu, safety glasses. Go to hell, you line, you. Argentina, I won't be crying for you. He imagines relaxing at home with legs stretched out, a can of beer in his hand. He won't have to wear steel-toed slippers to loaf around the house, won't need safety glasses to eat his lunch or help his wife do the dishes. On his walls, he can hang a couple of nudes by Modigliani or Renoir. He can puff a cigarette at any time. He can relax in his rocking chair without having to buckle up.

At times, he ponders his good luck. If the plant hadn't needed to reduce its workforce, he'd have been forced to vegetate here for at least five more years. He feels like a convict unexpectedly released for good behaviour. He is floating on the feeling that the most arduous phase of his life is coming to a close, that it will soon make way for a future of easier days. He has survived in relative health. He has made enough money to escape the reign of pragmatic *Must*, enough to slide into years ruled by the whimsical *May*. This summer he and his wife can take a trip to BC, or even the Yukon. They can travel for six weeks, or six months if they want to. There will be no sand sifting down in a mental hourglass marking off the hours until he has to report back.

With extraordinary diligence and a twinkle in his eye, he plans the first day of retirement. He'll set his alarm clock for five-thirty in the morning, and when it starts its tantrum, he'll smash it with a hammer. He'll keep on smashing and smashing until nothing, not even a tenth of a second, survives.

Three days left. Ambrose has trained his successor, so now they work half-hour-on, half-hour-off. It's just as well. It will get his body accustomed to less exertion and avert the shock of suddenly doing nothing. He spends his half-hours outside. Spring is yawning awake. He is no more than a step or two from leaving the tunnel of his drudgery. No more than two hundred and fifty, a hundred and twenty cars await him, then his Fordmate's hands and shoulders and back will relax, he'll let out a breath of relief, and he'll stride away from the plant toward his much-deserved rest.

A classical melody keeps playing in his mind, more often and more loudly now. He doesn't know or care that it's the last movement of Dvorak's Ninth Symphony, 'From the New World.' Maybe he heard it in a television commercial. Maybe it emanated from the windows of a car idling next to him at an intersection. Anyway, it matches his mood. Two more days. One more day. Then he'll be his own master—maybe good, maybe incompetent, but his own. Tomorrow, when he passes for the last time through the gate he's been entering and exiting for the past twenty-five years, that gate will become one-way only. He'll pass through for the final time, then drive home where he'll be welcomed by his wife with a hug and a kiss. Following the pop of a champagne cork, he *will* enter a new world. That triumphal music thundering in his inner ear is the soundtrack of a rejoicing soul.

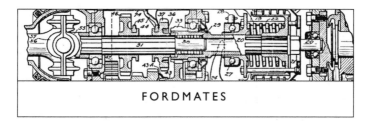

FORDMATES

After driving some fifteen kilometres south from London on High-way 4, you cross over Highway 401 and, turning slightly right, then left, descend the hump of the overpass to enter three kilometres of ruler-straight road: four lanes, a good surface, speed limit eighty kilometres per hour. During certain weekday hours—before seven in the morning and between three and four in the afternoon, cars here once routinely reached speeds of 120, even 140 kilometres per hour. That's why this stretch was nicknamed Ford's Raceway. In a minute, you pass the Flying M truckstop, then, just past that row of trees you are going to see … any moment now coming into view on the left … nothing? Where is it? There's nothing out there where the Ford plant should be! The plant has always been firmly planted here, but now I see nothing but horizon behind a chain-link fence.

Well, not quite nothing. Despite the grass and weeds pushing through cracks in the concrete, it's possible to identify the surface of the employee parking lot by the rusty guardrails still delineating the road to the main gate. There, behind the gate and the small security building, there should be—there used to be—the plant, a huge, sprawling factory, covering at least a square kilometre. From the tower above it, two blue ovals, Ford logos, looking in opposite directions, watched over the goings-on like all-seeing eyes, keeping a close watch on the plant that produced at least two hundred and fifty thousand cars each year. In the flat-roofed hall, three to four thousand people in blue coveralls calloused their hands and broke their backs. I used to be one of them. That plant, my plant, should be here, and it isn't. Is this field some type of mirage, playing tricks with my mind by hiding what I know must exist? Or was the mirage the plant where I used to work? Did I drive this highway five days a week for twenty-one years, or was it all a fantasy, an illusion? The highway is here, the parking lot is here, but where is the plant? Believe me, there once stood in this spot a huge hall full of rumbling, steel, sparks, hubbub, sweat, and beautiful cars. How can something so insubstantial as five years of time carry away something so absolutely, even brutally, substantial as a car assembly plant?

My head feels fuzzy. I'm dizzy. The backdrop, the witness of twenty-one years of my life, has disappeared. No witness, no line, no life? And yet, I drove here today in a car that was born in this plant many years ago. Where there is a car, there must be a plant. The car couldn't have simply materialized in this meadow, having assembled itself out of morning mist, oxygen, starlight, daisy fragrance, sunrays, and birdsong. No, I clearly remember the gang of us putting this car together, this one and thousands of others, part after part, line after line, hand after hand, until it took its first roaring breath at the end of line eight. That all happened. Take your eyes off a place for a few years, and suddenly, poof! It's gone.

But it's not gone, not really. Not completely. I don't have to close my eyes to see dozens of guns hanging above the line, silver bouquets of sparks, orange spirals of pressure hoses, grey chains or yellow jaws carrying frames, bodies, whole colourful cars. I can still hear the whistling, hissing, and screeching of the guns, the rattling of the line, the humming of ventilators, the clang of metal banging against metal, and all the snippets of talk and laughter and cursing of all those entrusted with that technology, who took it into their hands, lifted, carried, placed parts where they belonged, connected whatever had to be connected to enable a newborn car to come alive at the turn of a key, to charge off the line like a stallion let out to pasture, and head out for the roads of the world.

And today … no building obscures the morning sun, and no tower bearing the oval blue Ford eye keeps watch.

Assembly plants are built primarily of people. Take out the people and the whole empty structure of columns, rafters, and roof will collapse, either due to the ravages of time or the decisions of powerful accountants. In this case, the accountants were faster. The wrecking machines denied time the opportunity to sink its teeth into this plant. They've razed it all to the ground, everything but the concrete foundations. They've left time nothing to do but devour the parking lot. There, in the blue yonder behind the fence, a lonely stone-eating dinosaur grazes on the concrete and excretes gravel. The material evidence of my middle years has been knocked down, ground up, silenced. Now it exists only in those of us who laboured here for our daily bread. It's lodged in the memory department of our brains and in our muscles, vertebrae, joints, tendons, cartilage. The plant's signature on our bodies is indelible. Time will erase those marks only when it erases us.

How about a little walk around? With a bit of luck, we might figure out what the disappearing act is all about. This way used to lead to the main gate for the hourly employees. Behind those guardrails, which were grey before rust attacked them, the van pool vehicles used to park. There were up to forty of them at the peak of production. It was said that the company introduced them as an answer to the growing absenteeism of workers who liked to drink so much that they lost their driver's licences. Forbidden to drive, they couldn't make it to work. For a small fee, the company organized van pools to pick them up at home and bring them in. The service became popular even with people who could drive. I myself enjoyed riding the van pool for many years. I acted as substitute driver for a time. It was cheaper and more comfortable than driving your own car, and simpler, too. You didn't have to scrape ice off the windshield or clear the snow off in winter, and the van was always warm inside when it picked you up.

Besides hauling people to work, the van was a social club on wheels, not so much in the morning when everybody's mind was still operating at half speed, but the post-shift torrent of words was unstoppable. So much gossip from all corners of the factory, so many private victories and defeats the merry prattlers had to share! So many anecdotes of life's many petty surprises! For instance, we once waited ten minutes outside the house of an old boozer until his wife ran out the door in a nightgown to tell us that her Jack couldn't go in to work today. Next day Jack told us why: to forestall his evening trip to the pub, his wife had hidden his dentures, and in the morning couldn't remember where she'd put them. Another of our riders wasn't a drinker, but he was overly fond of pretty girls, and when he returned home from an assignation after midnight, his steady girlfriend beat him up so badly that she had to take him to emergency. For three days, he was unable to stand, let alone work. Compared to him she was a pipsqueak, but she must have been a very enraged pipsqueak. However, top prize for the most memorable event goes to a notorious boozer who had the golden touch when it came to bodywork. He could perform miraculous repairs, even when he could barely stand, his mind all but dissolved in alcohol. Because of the exceptional quality of his work, the Company tolerated his drinking and looked the other way when he had to curl up in the back seat of a car once in a while. After a little head-clearing nap, he'd continue applying his sheet metal wizardry. Once, this quiet passenger slumbered all the way to work, woke up just as we entered the parking lot, and in panic shouted at the driver: 'Jimmy, you forgot to pick me up!' Yes, we were transporting a good bunch of real characters. Where are they all now, I wonder.

Let's take a last walk through this place that now exists only in our memories, this rumbling, thundering space stretching almost beyond the reach of our eyes. On one side of the hall a thousand parts were once brought together, while on the other side, shiny cars of aristocratic breeding—Crown Victoria, Grand Marquis—emerged. Yes, let's go in before age completely dismantles our memory cells and leads us slowly towards the realm of oblivion.

My memory walks me in through the non-existent gate. In the locker room, I put on my coveralls and safety boots—even remembering can be dangerous, after all. I head towards the cafeteria. Passing the door to Medical reminds me that I have a file in there. I wasn't particularly prone to injury, but no one who works on or around an assembly line can avoid it completely. When a hoist fails and your hand is pinned to the line by an eight-cylinder engine, you end up at Medical through no fault of your own, counting your lucky stars your hand wasn't broken. And when you're kept on a killer job twice as long as anyone should be, it's no wonder you're ultimately diagnosed with tendinitis in your shoulder. When you work with solvents, you have to expect your fingers will suffer from burns.

Hurry to the cafeteria now. The girl with the dimples in her cheeks—the one who couldn't even get six inches out of the sixty feet of dicks on the line—sells you a cup of coffee. I've got the coffee cup in one hand and a cigarette in the other. Well, yes, a cigarette especially helps to bring back the plant as it was in my early days on the floor. Those days are imprinted deepest in my memory, maybe because I was more impressionable as a younger man, maybe because everything was so new and surprising, but probably because the factory had a much merrier atmosphere back then, and much more freedom.

I'm going to visit my old jobs, and recall the Fordmates who worked next to me. Odd that I know most of them only by their first name. One name is enough, I guess, just as it was for knights in the Middle Ages: Sir John, Sir James, Sir Galahad. The title, meant to guarantee their worthiness, elevated each of them into a select group of people. It was the same at Ford. The folks on each shift were fearless knights, scarred and steeled by skirmishes with the line. An elite club. I can precisely recall their faces, their movements on the line. I believe that I and all the others could still perform most of our jobs, should the imaginary line begin to move. Then again, there's no real line to prove me wrong. But two, three hundred thousand repetitions have lodged the moves in my muscle memory. The brain may forget, but the muscles remember. Which doesn't say much for the brain.

Right here, at the beginning of the chassis line, I spent a year and a half. This is the location of my initiation into Ford, my transformation from inmate to Fordmate. It is the place where I endured probation period, my worst torture on the job, and the place where my employment hung, for a few days, by a thread. I only survived thanks to my two pals. My partner on this two-man job employed his skill and deftness to make my half of the job as easy as possible. On a killer job, any relief is very welcome and sometimes vitally important. My partner knew that, and his efforts held my chin above water for those first two weeks, three weeks, when I was a breath away from drowning. Later, when we had worked together for only half a year, he offered to act as guarantor for a small loan, the down payment on my house. He offered solely on the basis of my performance at work, acting on an unwritten Ford ethic: show me how you work and I'll tell you who you are. When, years later, I thanked him for his help during my darkest hour, he just said, 'I'm sorry I couldn't do more.' There's a man of natural grandeur, a noble soul.

Right next to me, another gift and a morale booster, Captain Driveshaft, used to work. He was a lightning bolt of energy, an irrepressible source of creativity with a thirst for humour. He was a manufacturer of pranks. In spite of his killer job, he could always find the time to conceive and carry out a practical joke. I was a target a few times, but the pranks were always funny and never hurt.

He taught me that a bit of humour went a long way at Ford, that laughter is a potent antidote to monotony and boredom. Is he still out there making people laugh? Back then he played in an amateur rock group. I hope he's still playing, still spreading his joy for life.

This zone of the line was, for many years the domain of the supervisor for whom I worked several times. As a supervisor, he was a newbie, having come to Ford later in life after a previous career as a commercial pilot, but he was one of the best I encountered here. Most of the time, he was invisible, like some fairy-tale godfather, but whenever I turned on the light to call him, there he'd be, standing in front of me and solving my problem as if with a magical wand. Then, poof, he was gone again. He never stood behind my back, scrutinizing my work. He knew what was important. He was a good man who knew his place. I liked working for him.

Here is where a buddy of mine worked, breaking his back on steering boxes for who knows how many years. We were hired the same day, so our careers intertwined. While working ten-hour shifts at Ford, he managed to earn a university degree through correspondence courses. For two years, my job followed and completed his, so I could see and appreciate how well he did his job. He never sent me anything unfinished or screwed up, nothing to throw my job out of kilter. We had many good talks over cups of coffee. He'd read a lot, knew a lot. I hope he's enjoying his pension these days. He earned it.

This smiling gentleman approaching on his forklift is the driver of my van pool. He has well over thirty years of seniority under his belt. Years and years behind the controls of his forklift made him a real expert at handling material, and he was such a master that he was entrusted with training newbies in the skills of operating a forklift. An inquisitive man, he accumulated a wealth of knowledge about the Ford plant and the city of London, and he willingly shared stories of both from behind the wheel of the van.

For me, a newcomer to both London and the plant, these stories were priceless; they helped me to find my bearings, settle down. He retired three years before me, after almost thirty-seven years at work. I know he's enjoying his pension because we still meet up now and then.

I could keep going. I could keep introducing you to the whole crowd of extraordinary people I worked with here. Yes, extraordinary. I insist on the word. I don't like the phrase 'ordinary man,' or 'common man.' Those words betray the arrogance of those who use them, those who believe that only those with a university education or exalted social standing have rich, complex spiritual lives. That couldn't be further from the truth. More than a few folks with university degrees were working on those lines. Like my partner, some even earned a degree or two while toiling here. I could introduce you to a sculptor who works in wood. His masterpiece, a full-size and fully functional harp, is so beautiful that it's displayed in a museum. I worked with a man who was an archery champion before coming to Canada. In his best years, he was among the top twenty-five archers in the world. There was a writer, an immigrant, who wrote a book in his second language that was accepted by Canada's most prestigious publisher. It generated so much interest that the author spent two weeks giving interviews for radio, TV, and newspapers. Do you have any idea how many first-generation immigrants have worked here? Those people had to make the difficult decision to emigrate. Some, like the writer of that book, had to even create a secret plot to defect from their country behind the Iron curtain and come here as a refugee. The risks of emigration require uncommon character. Consider the dozens of entrepreneurial minds who managed to establish, almost overnight, an emergency supply network of food when the cafeterias were shut down. You could get almost everything the cafeterias offered, from coffee to soft drinks to sandwiches made to order and delivered into your hands just before lunch. This is not to mention the hundreds of workers pursuing their talents quietly at home, playing their instruments or painting or writing poetry, in private, just for their own pleasure. I hope you're not still thinking, if you ever did, that only 'ordinary' people worked here? So-called ordinary people would not have garnered for Mr Ford the silver, then even the gold J.D. Power Award, the most prestigious honour for an automotive assembly plant. Common folks, eh? Nope.

Well, our little walk is winding down. We've made it to my last day on the line. The end of the shift is near: one hundred and fifty more cars, forty more, six more, and here's a police cruiser, the last car I'll ever help to build. There's no feeling of triumph, though, no loud celebration that it's all behind me, that I've managed to survive my working years in relative health, that I've made enough money to last me for the rest of my days, that I can start the so-called perpetual holiday. There's a feeling of emptiness in the neighbourhood of my stomach. My days here weren't easy, but I spent about as much time here as I did at home. These lines became a second home that I inhabited for twenty-one years. My departure still hurts now, and why shouldn't it? I'm leaving dozens of people with whom I've become close, comfortable. There's no cause for celebration, even today.

I walk slowly toward the locker room. I dress in my 'civilian' clothes, empty my locker, dawdle across the yard to the gate. I'm moving reluctantly, as if I've had a change of heart, as if I'm afraid of walking through the gate one last time only to enter some new, unfamiliar life. Leaving the plant feels, again, like shedding some protective shell, like ceasing to be a Fordmate. No wonder I'm anxious. But that's wrong. Once a Fordmate, always a Fordmate. After all, my memories are more durable than the plant.

It is as if the whole factory has followed my steps and passed through some gate into the next phase of its existence. That whole structure, the hundreds of steel columns and rafters, is gone, disassembled and delivered to a scrap yard. It must have taken long processions of trucks. All that retired steel, melted down and forged into something new, maybe some new assembly plant. Who knows, perhaps that steel has a memory of its own. Maybe something of Ford will remain, something of our atmosphere, our work, our existence.

Well, well, well. That plant of ours isn't here. It's almost as if it never had been, as if I'd dreamed it up. Have I dreamed up my whole life? No, I'm just letting my thoughts go free. I still carry the plant in my aches and pains. The plant bought the house I live in. I still drive one of the cars we made. I enjoy my Ford benefits package. The plant is like those long-extinguished stars whose light is only just now reaching us, and will keep reaching us as long as we live.

There should be some memorial plaque here, like the kind one finds at historic places like the Oregon trail, or important portages on Hudson Bay Company canoe routes. A memorial or some kind of gravestone. Just a little something to announce to pilgrims that a Ford assembly plant existed here, that for forty-four years it produced over ten million cars and employed over fifteen thousand workers. Those workers deserve a memorial, something tangible to visit, to anchor their memories. But it might be too much to expect a memorial to be erected by an empty field.

Or maybe that former Fordmate, the writer, will someday write a book of his memories. Maybe he will build us a little memorial out of words, a little something for all of us who spent our days and nights out here and are proud Fordmates still.

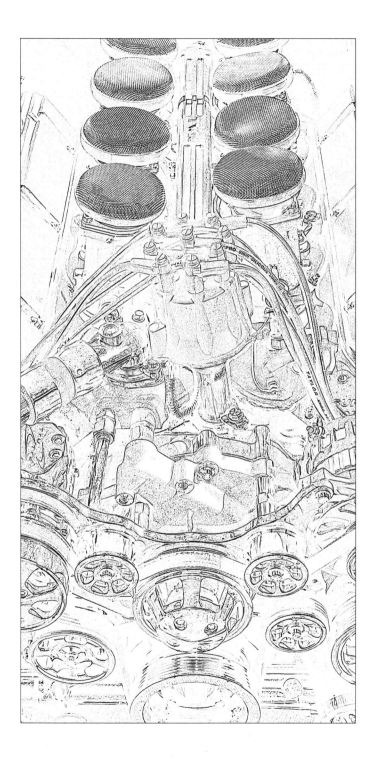

ACKNOWLEDGEMENTS

A big thank-you goes to Stan Dragland for being the perfect editor for this collection of stories and for his unwavering thirty-years-long support of my writing career.

For additional editorial suggestions and fine tuning the manuscript for publication, I am indebted to Stephanie Small.

I also thank Jean McKay for helping me to refine my vocabulary by suggesting the right words or idioms that are hard or impossible to find in a dictionary.

Jim Stewart, a veteran of St. Thomas Assembly Plant, helped me with the technical terminology related to assembling cars. Thank you, Jim.

And finally, my biggest thanks go to my family, my wife, Jana, and son, Ivo, for being with me while I was living this book and when I was writing it, indeed, for every day of the years we've been together.

Among the stories inspired by Ford, I wrote one that didn't quite match the spirit of others and I decided not to publish it in this book. However, I believe that it is a funny story that might entertain you. If you are interested, you can find and read 'Fateful Night' at www.moravecbooks.com.